80#

PAAMON

PRESS

PAAMON
PRESS

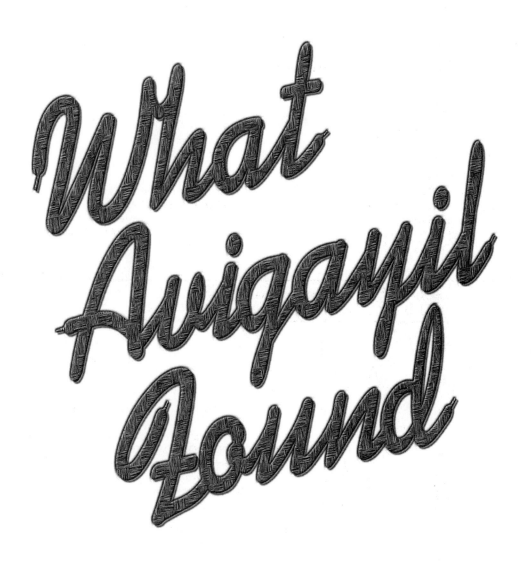

# What Avigayil Found

A Novel By
**Miriam L. Elias**

FIRST EDITION
*First Impression … May 2000*

Published by
**PAAMON PRESS**

Distributed by
**MESORAH PUBLICATIONS, LTD.**
4401 Second Avenue / Brooklyn, N.Y 1123

Distributed in Europe by
**J. LEHMANN HEBREW BOOKSELLERS**
20 Cambridge Terrace
Gateshead, Tyne and Wear
England NE8 1RP

Distributed in Israel by
**SIFRIATI / A. GITLER**
10 Hashomer Street
Bnei Brak 51361

Distributed in Australia and New Zealand by
**GOLDS BOOK & GIFT SHOP**
36 William Street
Balaclava 3183, Vic., Australia

Distributed in South Africa by
**KOLLEL BOOKSHOP**
Shop 8A Norwood Hypermarket
Norwood 2196, Johannesburg, South Africa

ISBN:
1-57819-546-2 (hard cover)
1-57819-547-0 (paperback)

Typography by CompuScribe at ArtScroll Studios, Ltd.
Printed in the United States of America by Noble Book Press Corp.
Bound by Sefercraft, Quality Bookbinders, Ltd., Brooklyn N.Y. 11232

*Dedication -*

*This book is dedicated to our darling
great grandchildren, with love and hugs.*

# Acknowledgments

My sincerest thanks to all those who who helped in so many different ways in the writing of this book; most especially, **Rabbi Shmuel & Esther Wenger, Chumi Eisemann, Rivky Grodziasky, Delli Katzenstein, Sora Chaitovsky,** and **Channa Baum,** for giving so generously of their precious time and expertise.

*Yeyasher Kochachem!*

כשם שאין פרצופותיהן
דומין זה לזה,
כך אין דעתם שוין זה לזה

*Just as people's features*
*are not exactly like one another's,*
*so their personalities are not exactly alike.*

(מדרש רבה)

כבד את ה' מהונך - מאשר חננך

*Honor Hashem with your wealth -*
*with whatever He has granted you.*

(ילקוט משלי ג')

# *Part One*

# *Chapter One*

**S**he clutched it in one hand, wedged between other letters, several flyers, and some junk mail, with no inkling of what she was holding or what it would come to mean in her life. With her chin clamped down on the letters to prevent their slipping, she used her other hand to fasten the storm door, and then the house door, against the icy black night.

"Anything interesting for a change?" Her mother, already busy in the kitchen with the post-Shabbos cleanup, sounded dubious.

Avigayil dumped the pile of mail onto the coffee table and fanned out the letters.

"Nothing much here," she called out, trying to make herself heard above the sound of running water. "A bar mitzvah invitation, the yeshivah newsletter, flyers for Macy's and A&P, bills ... oh, wait! Here's something from South Africa! Wow, nice stamp!" She picked up the legal-sized envelope and brought it to her mother.

Mrs. Kaplan straightened up from loading the dishwasher, and, wiping her hands on the little terry towel attached to her apron, peered at the letter.

"What's that all about?" she mumbled. "Who knows us in Johannesburg? It's some kind of law firm: 'Benton, Cox and Green, Jr., Solicitors.' Probably something to do with Tatty's new project at work, though why they'd send it here and not to the office beats me. The mail isn't usually very exciting ... I can't imagine why we run downstairs every week the minute Shabbos is over, just in case. It's always the same old stuff."

She sighed and turned back to cleaning the counters. "Put the *Havdalah* things together, please," she called over her shoulder. "Tatty'll be home in a minute."

Avigayil added the letter to the pile, and as she set up the candle, cup, *besamim* box and matches, she thought about South Africa. It's summer there now, she mused; that's hard to believe. I'd hate to have Chanukah in the middle of a heat wave, but I guess everyone's used to things the way they live them.

"Hi! *Gut Voch!*" Shuli, flushed and sparkling, dashed up the stairs, bringing a freezing gust of wind in her wake.

"So where've you been so long? I need help around here!" said Mrs. Kaplan.

"I went home with Chaya Sarah after Bnos, and stayed to study for mid-terms." Shuli flung her coat and scarf over a chair. "Her braces are coming off this week, just in time for Nachum's *chasunah*. Great timing, no? What's there for me to do?" She slumped down on the couch as if too exhausted to wait for forthcoming orders. "Hey, Avi, how come you didn't go to Chany's house? I saw the whole ninth grade piling in there right after Bnos, but not you."

Avigayil shrugged her shoulders and clamped her mouth shut. It was none of Shuli's business.

"What are you doing tonight?" she asked, switching the focus back to her sister.

"Chaya Sarah's mother said we could have the kitchen to ourselves tonight and we're going to bake for the *Aufruf*. They've bought a whole bunch of molds that were on special, so we can make some gorgeous chocolate creations, too. We'll have a blast! And you?"

"Nothing." Avigayil shrugged again. It was becoming quite a habit. "Oh! I hear the car. That's Tatty," she said.

Mr. Kaplan was the president of the small *shul* they attended, and there were always dozens of reasons why he had to remain there longer than anyone else. A tall, heavy man, he took charge and accepted responsibility as naturally as others preferred to dodge such burdens. Whether in his home, his business or his *shul*, he was ruler, but he was nevertheless loved and respected by family and employees alike, due to his unique kindness and deep understanding in all his dealings.

"*Gut Voch!*" his voice boomed. "Sorry I'm late, but I had to set up for tomorrow's breakfast meeting with the building committee. The plans are really coming along, *baruch Hashem*. Soon it'll be time to enlist the ladies. What do you say, Sue?"

"I couldn't care less about colors for carpets and bathroom tiles," his wife answered, as she came into the dining room and sat down at the table to hear *Havdalah*. "But when you're up to planning the kitchen I certainly have some ideas of my own. The way things are now you can't have more than two ladies working side by side without bumping into each other constantly. And the mess! There's nowhere to put anything. It's awful!"

"That's what our *minyan's* famous for, real togetherness." Mr. Kaplan laughed and began to pour the wine. Avigayil held the candle and Shuli shut the light. Their father's beautiful voice filled the room, and then they joined him in singing *Hamavdil* and *Eliyahu HaNavi*. Mr. Kaplan often acted as *baal tefillah* in addition to his other duties in *shul*. He frequently remarked that all Kaplans sang — it was in their genes, he insisted, a birthright — and it was true. They loved to sing, and were adept at impromptu harmonizing.

Some hours later, with Shuli fast asleep in the twin bed next to hers, Avigayil, still tossing and turning, thought she heard her parents mention her name.

'They never analyze Shuli,' she mused. 'They're always concerned and upset about me. I wish they wouldn't worry so much. Not everyone has to have millions of friends. I'm okay the way things are. I wish they'd all just leave me alone.'

ଏଞ୍ଚ ଏଞ୍ଚ ଏଞ୍ଚ

The next day, Sunday, Avigayil got home from school at one o'clock. There was no sign of Shuli; she had probably stayed on for Clubs. Making her way through to the little sewing room off the kitchen, Avigayil called:

"Hi, Ma! How's it coming?"

"Hi, Avi!" Mrs. Kaplan looked up from her work and smiled. "I think you'll like it," she said. "The skirt's almost finished, see?" She held up a navy blue garment, shot through with faint markings of burgundy. "It's the most delicious fabric I've worked with for the longest time. Maybe I'll make you two vests; one like the skirt, and one all burgundy." She removed her glasses and stretched. "Phew! I've been sewing for about two hours; I can't believe it. Let's have lunch, and after we've eaten, I have a surprise for you!"

"A surprise?" Avigayil sounded skeptical. It was probably another of the many plans hatched for her 'entertainment' or social life in general. "Why does it have to wait until after lunch? I just can't bear the suspense," she said sarcastically.

"This one's worth waiting for, I promise," said her mother. "Grilled cheese sandwiches for two?"

The kitchen was awash with bright winter sunshine. Avigayil, munching on her favorite sandwich, found herself relaxing in the warmth of the moment, her mother close by sipping a cup of hot tea, and seemingly occupied with her own thoughts. For once there were no questions as to how her morning had gone or what her plans were for the afternoon. What bliss!

She reached for the bowl of fruits, taking one clementine and rolling it across the table toward her mother; then she began peeling another for herself. Perhaps now was a good time to have it all out, she thought.

"Were you and Tatty discussing me again last night? I wasn't listening on purpose, honest! But I'm almost sure I heard my name come up."

"We'll just have to improve our whispering techniques," her mother smiled. She stood and began collecting the cutlery and glasses. "What else did you hear?"

"Nothing really." Avigayil looked up at her mother with a pleading face. "I wasn't trying to listen in, but I've just gotten to the point where I'm almost waiting for it by now. I know you're worried about me, and, like, I haven't managed to convince you that I'm really okay!"

"Why don't you *bentch*," said Mrs. Kaplan, "and then I'll give you your surprise. It may answer your questions about last night. And then some!" she added with great emphasis.

# Chapter Two

"Okay, here it is," announced Mrs. Kaplan, handing an envelope to Avigayil. "That letter from South Africa wasn't for Tatty after all; it's for you. Why don't you go into your room and take your time reading it? Judging from the thickness it will take you some time!"

"Have you read it? Do you know what it's about?" asked Avigayil.

"No and yes. We have not read this letter to you, but there was an enclosure for us, and so we know the gist of it." She gave Avigayil's shoulder a gentle squeeze and shoved her in the direction of the girls' bedroom. "Go ahead, it won't bite!" she urged, and turned to answer the ringing telephone.

Avigayil sat on her bed and pulled the heavy sheaf of pages out of the large envelope. Slowly, she began to read.

> *Dear Avigayil,*
>
> *I am writing to you from my little flat on the top floor of an old house, on a winding street in a remote area just north of Johannesburg, South Africa. So much for that! It's where I've lived for the past twenty years, more or less; at peace with myself. It's a retreat of sorts from my other life, which was turbulent and often unbearably sad. I work part-time, in a one-room library, which is housed in back of the local post office, so that to an extent I am still in touch with humanity, and not a complete recluse. Sometimes the temptation is strong to have my few groceries delivered to the house and retire from the job, the world in general, and sit rocking at the window under the slanting roof, gaze over the tree tops into the distance, and just reminisce.*
>
> *But not yet! To you, my child, I want to explain how it all came about, and why I have turned to you at this time. Your name is Avigayil, as was our mother's ...but let me begin at the beginning.*

Avigayil lay back against her pillow and wriggled into a comfortable position, completely absorbed in what she was reading. Who was this person, and what could she possibly have to say to her?

> *You see, I'm Doreen Silver, the long-lost oldest sister of your grandmother Babsie (short for Barbara). There were seven of us: Solly, myself, Leonard and*

Sidney, Daisy, Leon and Babsie. Our father was a tailor on Commercial Road in the East End of London, England, and we lived right above the shop.

Our hard-working parents were worn to the bone, just keeping us clothed and fed. The flat, mostly freezing cold and shabby altogether, had a dank, gray aura about it, brightened only by the little bunch of flowers my mother always managed to scrounge or beg from the flower vendor down the street. Mum had a passion for flowers, and was starved for the sight and smell of them in that dreary, drab environment of brick and cobbled stone. Many's the time she bartered some odds and ends — buttons and threads from our father's shop, or even a home-baked challah — for a bunch of sweet peas or pansies. It was like a mini-pool of sunlight in the center of the kitchen table, that posy of flowers, stuck in an old jam jar. It was her stab at ... self-hood? Is there such a word?

I have years of memories of our father, even though small and slight, having to duck under the ever-present damp nappies (now known as diapers, and disposable) strung on a pulley line suspended from the ceiling, above the fireplace. They would drip, then gradually go from semi-dry to hard, rough and stiff, when they'd be taken down to be replaced by the next batch.

The smells were all-pervading inside, and even out. We lived between the Tate and Lyle sugar factory on one end of the street, and the Beecham Liver Pills factory on the other. The sickly sweetness on the left subtly mingled with the strong aroma of rotting veggies from the right, seeping through the cracks and crannies of our old house, and swirling about our heads when we stepped outside.

*The biggest treat was the kosher fish and chips shop next door, where you bought hot, tasty snacks wrapped in newspaper. We usually ate these on the way home, unable to wait another minute for the crackly pungent delight.*

*On Shabbos, Daisy and I went to the shul around the corner, where our father was the gabbai. It was a rather old but quite impressive building, with a women's gallery upstairs, replete with a wrought- iron grille mechitzah. Our mother stayed home with the little ones, but I do remember taking turns with her on Yom Kippur. On Simchas Torah, of course, even the babies came along, and our father dispensed sweets as if money rained down in torrents from the sky over our house on Commercial Road.*

Avigayil took a deep breath and stared at the batch of paper that was piling up next to her. It was like a story from an exciting book. Her mind flew to Bubby Babsie, clearly picturing her lying in a little wooden cradle, covered up to her tiny pink nose to keep her warm, staring up at the drying diapers above her head. Why hadn't she ever told them anything about her childhood in London? Probably because nobody had asked. The name Doreen had certainly never been mentioned in this house. She sniffed the good clean air in the room, and felt immensely rich. Snuggling back amongst the pillows, she continued to read.

*The boys attended the Jewish Secondary School in North London. It was understood they were due a proper Jewish education, whereas we girls were given Hebrew lessons in a cheder, three afternoons a week, with a lady teacher. She wasn't bad as I remember;*

*kind and devoted to her task, but the whole thing lacked luster, mystery or joy.*

*During the day, we attended Prince Edward School for Primary, and Fairclough St. School for Secondary education. Strange as it may seem, most of the children, and many teachers at these schools, were Jewish.*

*Some of my friends were considerably better off than we were, and their fathers came to our shop to be measured for suits. They respected Daddy's expertise and unfailing honesty. They got what they paid for, fair and square, and always beautifully tailored at that!*

*In my class, I longed to have the blond, shoulder-length corkscrew curls of a girl named Angela. I pined for the shiny brown shoes she wore to school, burnished to a deep brown luster like the horse chestnuts we loved (and called conkers).*

*She, of the huge satin bow at the back of her head; she, for whose company girls groveled and fought. Angela March, whose friends could be bribed to let you tag along on their walks if you produced the right currency. For instance, providing the correct answers to the arithmetic homework due for the next day would allow you to stroll with them through the park; two sets of answers, as far as an excursion to the nearby Tower of London.*

What else is new, Avigayil wondered. Different times, different names, but basically, nothing's changed. Poor Doreen! Why didn't she just retreat and close herself off? It could be done, Avigayil knew.

*Of course there was no bathtub in our flat, and we were all dispatched to the public baths every Thursday* night, to usher in Shabbos squeaky-clean. But prior to this, it was my weekly lot, starting from the age of nine, to choose carefully and bargain hard for the Shabbos chicken, and drag it, alive and squawking, to the shochet, to be killed and plucked. This I did for many years, and while our mother soaked and salted my prey, I too soaked in the public baths, where the strong smell of carbolic soap and disinfectant, mixed with the hiss and belching of hot water pipes, produced a languor and near stupor that I can still conjure up at a moment's notice at the age of seventy-eight! I chuckle, too, when I recall how my brothers Lenny and Sidney used their bath pennies for toffees at the sweet shop, and most of the time managed to scrub enough grime off their necks and behind their ears to fool our mother.

The Baron Settlement, a 'free' after-school club sponsored by the London County Council, was our only source for legally acquired gastronomic delights. When the last school bell rang at four o'clock, we flew through those few streets, like messenger pigeons released from their loft cages, to the Settlement house. Hot cocoa, biscuits and sugared buns awaited us there, all free and strictly kosher (in special consideration for the many observant children of the poor). This wonderful treat was followed by a variety of activities in clubs which we could join at random, and thus pass our time until our trek home in the chilly dusk, street lamps flickering on, one by one, to guide us along the way.

Homework was a push-and-shove affair at the kitchen table, perennially covered by a shiny, cracked piece of oilcloth, the air thick with lingering smells of *fried kipper. Sometimes one or two of my friends would come over, and we would crowd into the frigid girls' bedroom to study our poetry and Shakespeare, huddled together on the big double bed that belonged to Daisy and me. Babsie still slept on a small cot under the window. She was only five when I was fifteen and studying for my matric the following year, 1939.*

*In May, '39, just before my 16^(th) birthday, we received a letter that turned my life around. It was an invitation from our uncle, our father's older brother, for me to come and spend the summer with his family in America. Uncle Berel was a widower, living with his married daughter — my cousin Sara — and her husband and two small children. Uncle Berel, also a tailor by trade (both sons having been apprenticed to their father, a master tailor from the old country, early in life) still worked daily in the employ of a classy establishment in the city. His two sons were younger than Sara, and away at university at the time.*

*His letter went something like this:*

Doreen must be taking her Matriculation now. As a special treat, and as a reward for passing with flying colors, of which I have no doubt, I have decided to send you this return ticket to have her spend her vacation here with us. We hope you will give your permission and we look forward greatly to seeing her. It's such a shame that we live so far apart; after all, *there are only the two of us!* We really must make the effort not to drift entirely apart. So please confirm as soon as possible. We'll have her home in time to begin whatever you have planned for her to do next year.

All our love, Berel

*The exhilaration on Commercial Road knew no bounds. Even Angela, of the golden curls, fell under the marvelous spell of a classmate actually going to another continent, and glittering America at that! She wheedled me into moving into the desk next to hers while we sat for our exams, and her conspiratorial smiles aimed my way every once in a while made my head swell. I wrote my papers in a fever of excitement, the answers and ideas simply coming to me as if they were beamed directly into my brain. Pages and pages just piled up, covered in fluent script by my brand-new fountain pen, as we switched from Math to English; from French to History. There was no let-up to my adrenalin.*

*When the results came in, I had done even better than I'd expected. My parents were proud, my brothers and sisters were delighted, and I was in a state of euphoria.*

*In another week I would be on my way.*

*Like a runner at the starting line, I strained for that whistle: go, Doreen, GO!*

Avigayil sat up and rubbed her eyes. The telephone rang and a door slammed somewhere in the house. She looked about her room as if to touch base with reality. She was still holding several pages, and she knew that these must contain the threads that would somehow connect her to this story of the past, and the sixteen-year-old girl, Doreen Silver. Once more she settled into a comfortable position and resumed reading.

*To whom it may concern:*
*I regret to have to inject myself at this point, but shortly before her passing, Ms. Silver came to our*

office to request that the next eleven pages of her letter to you be shredded, and therefore omitted from the document. She substituted the following few pages. (Edward Cox)

Dear Avigayil, I have decided to cover the next sixty-two years of my life in a short resume. On careful consideration, I decided to take my secrets along with me. No good can come of telling and revealing, excusing and justifying.

Let me just say that when I arrived in the States, I learned that my uncle had, only two days earlier, died from a sudden massive heart attack. It was a terrible shock to his family, and none of them were too excited about the prospect of entertaining this unknown little cousin from England for the next few weeks. In their grief, understandably, they had very little room for me. They allowed me to wander about and explore on my own, but nevertheless, always made me feel that my home was with them. They had become rather acclimated to their host country at the expense of their observance of Judaism, and even Shabbos bore hardly any resemblance to what I knew from London.

So wander I did. I drifted and traveled, finally distancing myself from them altogether. In September of 1939, England declared war on Germany, and although the USA was not in the fray until much later, travel across the ocean became almost impossible.

I stayed, and for many years I studied, working my way through college. Having always loved books above all else, I eventually became a librarian. I cut off all contact with home, because I was too ashamed — and yes, cowardly — to own up to my guilt as a non-

*observant Jew. As year followed upon year, the prospect of facing my family became harder and harder until I admitted to myself that I just could never climb that particular mountain.*

*As a Peace Corps volunteer, I finally ended up in South Africa, where I decided to put down new roots. Thank G-d, I have returned to our beliefs. I have come around full circle, and have been an observant Jew for many years, but it came too late, alas, for our parents to have known. I will carry the heavy burden of this with me all the rest of my life.*

*And now, my very dear Avigayil, you will wonder, what's all this to do with me? I'll explain. I have decided to leave the bulk of my estate to various Jewish charities. But since I lack descendants, I wish, in addition, to leave the sum of $5000 to every one of my parent's great-grandchildren that are named after them. And you, of course, are one of these.*

"Whoa!" Avigayil's eyes widened as she read over the last paragraph once again. "$5000! Is this for real?" Her hands gripped the remaining page as she raced through the rest.

*In Velvel Kaplan's family, you are the one,* the letter continued. *And, as you probably know, there are quite a number of Velvels and Avigayils in Manchester, England and also in Eretz Yisrael. But since my youngest sister, Babsie, had only one son, your father Velvel, and your parents have two daughters, you are the only child in the States to receive this bequest.*

Avigayil noticed that her hands shook so badly, she had trouble reading. She placed the last page on the bed, and studied the final paragraph.

*YOU are to decide what to do with this money. It*

is entirely yours to spend on whatever your heart desires. I have only one stipulation: Permit your Grandma Babsie to approve your wishes. This is to make sure that you do not waste or squander the money on foolishness. I have the feeling that she will know best whether your investment, in whatever you choose, would have pleased our mother and would have made her happy. However, in the end, it's really all up to you!

Think kindly of me, if you can —

With love, your great-aunt, Doreen

# Chapter Three

The $5000 check, issued by a bank in Johannesburg, became the main focus of all subsequent dinner conversations around the Kaplans' table. A close runner-up was the amazing story of Doreen, who had never, ever been alluded to by their grandmother, Babsie. In fact, even now, Bubby Kaplan was very tight-lipped about the whole thing. All she would say was, "Yes, Doreen was the oldest and she left the rest of us for whatever she thought was best for herself." And when pressed further, she added, "After some years, when her rare post cards stopped coming altogether, we children learned to come to terms with the idea that she really wanted to make a clean break of it. I think she must have regretted her choice a million times, but not enough to go home. Mummy and Daddy never gave up hope that one fine day Doreen would be back on our doorstep, asking their forgiveness and explaining it all. It broke their hearts."

"It's an incredible journey she took," commented Mr. Kaplan, shaking his head. "A far, far trek from the frum family in pre-war London's East End. But, you know, in a sense she did come home in the end. Those first sixteen years of her life were the strong magnet that finally drew her back to *Yiddishkeit*."

But now that the floodgates had been opened, Bubby couldn't let it go at that.

"She left our parents with the six of us, and then they lost Solly in the War of Independence in *Eretz Yisrael*," she sighed deeply.

"Those two oldest children, I suppose, were looking for excitement and adventure, things that we were just a little short of in the East End. Solly secretly volunteered, and then informed our parents that he was off to help fight in Palestine, as it was called then. He was twenty-six years old, and a real doer! The Zionists smuggled him over there, but he was killed in action almost immediately. And even for Solly's *shivah* Doreen didn't come back."

Avigayil and Shuli couldn't get enough of it. This was real-life drama. It certainly beat the fictitious melodramatics of the yearly major play in Bais Yaakov.

"Still, it's wrong to talk bad about anyone, and that includes a person who's already in the next world. She did suffer plenty, with little enough *nachas*. And, as you said, Velvel, she did real *teshuvah* in the end." Bubby had no more to add.

"Maybe she never even knew about Solly?" Shuli ventured.

"Maybe," said Bubby, "but I rather doubt it. There's a secret someone who must have been in touch with her all these years. Otherwise, for one thing, how would she know about all these Avigayils and Velvels?"

That new piece of conjecture made things even more intriguing.

At night in bed, the various possibilities were further explored by the girls. Shuli, who was still reeling from the blow of having been named after their mother's side of the family, wavered between positive and negative reactions to the astounding news.

"No fair," she'd wail one night. "And no one even called her Avigayil. Bubby says she was always known as Abby: Abby Silver. Oh, what's the difference? You're just the lucky one. What're you going to do with all this loot? How about sharing some of it with poor little me?"

Avigayil, who was still trying to convince herself that all this was actual fact and not a dream, was as quiet and uncommunicative as ever.

"First I'll give *maaser* — that's $500. Can you believe it? I want to decide exactly where that should go. Mommy said she'll put the rest in the bank; you know, open a special account for me, so I'll have plenty of time to make up my mind. Right now, I'm still in total shock! And after all, what's the rush?"

"Let's do some brainstorming anyway. Hey! You could go to camp all summer this year. You've never been at a sleep-away camp in your entire life!"

This was followed by a prolonged silence, and then —

"Don't wanna. Never did."

Shuli couldn't give up, not yet.

"So go to *Eretz Yisrael*, and England, and meet all the other honored Avigayils and Velvels. I'd even be willing to tag along to entertain you on the flight, and to be useful in lots of little ways. Like booking sightseeing tours, and shopping for clothes and gifts. I sure would miss the bungalow colony, and my day camp job, but to help you out, I'd sacrifice," she giggled.

"Oh, go to sleep," Avigayil mumbled and yawned, turning her back on Shuli and burrowing in under her covers. "I'll come up with something — sooner or later."

During the day things were not much different. All news travels fast, good and bad, and Avigayil soon found out that this was no exception.

With the speed of light, the story of her inheritance was passed from mouth to mouth, and with each telling the details became embellished more and more. The exact sum of money involved already ran into the millions, and Great-aunt Doreen had undergone so many transformations, her own family wouldn't have recognized her. This, of course, wasn't that far off from the truth.

The curiosity about the circumstances surrounding the bequest was only matched by the unceasing speculation on how it would be spent.

"After all, it's not $500.00 we're talking about," stated Avigayil's classmate Mindy, to a small group gathered at her house, with the air of one who knew exactly how much had been bequeathed.

"It makes a good game," said Yehudis. "Go around the room and ask everyone what they would do if they got that lucky."

And the funniest part was that when they were actually confronted with the question, and tried to be serious about answering truthfully, none of them came up with very original ideas: Taking trips around the world, or perhaps a whole summer in camp, and of course, enormous shopping sprees prior to either of those, or in any case. Naturally, they also had various ideas about giving *tzedakah*, helping out some of those worthy cases so often described in the Jewish newspapers.

Mindy was sure she'd take private lessons in accordion. "It's my dream," she murmured, raising her eyebrows and sighing deeply.

"It's hard to imagine what Avi will spend it on. She hasn't really ever wanted anything much," said Perel. "Who knows; she's deep!"

And they went on to discuss the more mundane topics of their everyday lives.

Occasionally, even a teacher or friend of the Kaplans would come right out and ask Avigayil what she planned to do, or how she felt about it all. And the girl's quiet but firm answer was always the same. She was overwhelmed, but had decided to put the money into a savings account and wait to decide what she really wanted. So far, she had given *maaser*, with the help of her parents, and as for the rest, she had no clue.

# *Chapter Four*

**T**hey were on their yearly pilgrimage to the Piney Hollow Bungalow Colony. Avigayil stared out at the passing scenery, absently rubbing her shinbone where one leg of her mother's easel kept digging into her flesh. The car was loaded to within an inch of its life, and changing positions was more trouble than it was worth. The rain was relentless, drumming on the roof and pelting the side windows. The windshield wipers flipped and flopped without letup, beating time to the latest *Regesh* tape cheerfully playing, accompanied by her father's exuberant sing-along.

'I wish I were more like Tatty,' thought Avigayil. 'He's definitely the most positive person I've ever met. It's such a gloomy, yukky day — we have to drive another hour in this flood, unload seven thousand things and get them into the bungalow before they disintegrate, make beds, and it's probably below zero in there from the whole winter, and of course the toilet won't work — and he's singing away! I bet Mommy's not exactly delirious with joy. Probably she's panicking about Tatty's driving too fast, and wishing a miracle would happen to stop the rain and conjure up a brilliant burst of sunshine for our arrival at Piney.'

"How many years have we been coming here, Ma?" asked Shuli. "Six or seven years?"

"More than that," said Mrs. Kaplan. "The Brinkmans bought this place when you were a baby, and that's when we decided we'd all be better off in the country than in sticky New York. We were among the pioneers there. Don't you remember those photos of yourself in the playpen in front of the cottage? We have them all in the basement in the great big picture box. You know something, kids? You were both delicious back then, and no one ever talked back!"

"We've been in the same place for too long," grumbled Shuli. "We need a change. Next summer I'm going to *Eretz Yisrael* as Avi's personal maid. Okay, Avi? We'll stick it out one more year in Crummy Hollow, and next July we'll be on our way."

Avigayil said nothing. Everything looked as if a gigantic wet paintbrush had been coating the entire landscape in a translucent gray. Houses, trees and grass, buildings, and malls, cars and gas stations all retained their colors, but under an immense gauze-like drapery of pearl-gray. The only stark contrast was the ivory-black glistening asphalt of the highway.

"By the way, I'm sleeping on the single bed," she said suddenly.

"I don't care," Shuli sounded as if she really didn't. "As long as you promise to let me come along next summer. But no promise — and *I* sleep in the single bed."

"Shuli, you're crazy. Nobody's going to *Eretz Yisrael*, and I have the bed. I said it first and that's it!"

Avigayil rarely made waves, but when she got angry or was set on something, there was no arguing with her. Shuli, with a deep, exaggerated sigh, settled in her corner and closed her eyes.

Avigayil, somewhat surprised at her easily won victory, scratched her sore leg and searched for something soft she could wedge between the poking easel and her long-suffering shinbone. Ah, there! Dangling from the easel's crossbar was a plastic shopping bag, stuffed with assorted rags her mother had brought along for cleaning her brushes and other jobs around the house. That would be perfect! Avigayil fished out a piece of her old pink flannel pajamas. The heavenly relief was instantaneous. Why couldn't she have thought of it before?

"I guess the Neufelds will be there again, Ma, right?" she asked her mother, in the passenger seat in front of her.

"I expect so," said Mrs. Kaplan. "It's a good place for Esti, and she's used to it. The summer must be a hard time for her anyhow with no real routine or structure. At least she's been coming since she was a baby, so it's not a scary, threatening place for her."

'She must be about six now,' thought Avigayil. It seemed to her that Esti's life was one big chain forged of struggles. It was as if there were a constant measuring of goals achieved or missed, an unrelenting pressure to learn and improve in skills that came to other people as naturally as breathing.

"I wish they would all lay off and let her relax for a while in the summer months." She talked into her mother's right ear, above the clickety clack of the windshield wipers and her father's vocal renditions.

"It's not all that simple," her mother answered. "That would not necessarily be doing her a favor. The more she learns, the easier life will be for her in the long run. And marking time usually means regressing. Mrs. Neufeld is really wonderful with Esti, and it can't be easy with all those other kids. I think they just had a new little boy around Chanukah." Mrs. Kaplan peered ahead and squinted into the distance. "Oh, yes!" She sounded positively triumphant. "There's the traffic light ahead. We'll be there in five minutes."

๑෯๑ ๑෯๑ ๑෯๑

On Tuesday morning everything was in its place. They had unloaded the car Sunday afternoon in the downpour, and Mr. Kaplan had driven back to the city at six o'clock the next morning. It had taken the best part of yesterday to settle in, a process that was constantly interrupted by old friends dropping by to say hello, or to borrow this or that. But today, in the bright sunshine, it seemed to Avigayil as if they'd never left here at the end of last summer. The day camp was already in full swing with its different groups scattered over the grounds. Shuli, in the far distance, was supervising some kind of circle game with the six-year-olds. This afternoon the pool would be open and ready for use. She couldn't wait to dive in!

"Avi," her mother called from the back of the bungalow.

Avigayil roused herself from the glider and stretched. She ambled down the three narrow steps and around the side of the bungalow to the picnic table in the rear. Her mother was sorting her index cards of recipes. Avigayil grinned. She knew that one of her mother's projects for this summer was to re-write and organize all her recipes, which at this point were a jumble of stained cards and odd scraps of paper. It would be a long, boring job, but she was amused at how quickly and resolutely her mother had gotten down to tackling it.

"I see you've started in on this miserable business already," she said.

"If I push it off, I'll always think of another excuse to get out of it," sighed Mrs. Kaplan. "Believe me, it's not one minute too soon. This box is a disaster area." She began arranging piles. "Listen, Avi: Mrs. Brinkman wants to give you a job."

"A job?"

"Yes. She asked whether I think you'd like to help them out; something to do with grocery orders. Why don't you go down to the main house, and see what it's all about?" Mrs. Kaplan turned back to shuffling her cards and peering at their spotty contents.

"Okay, may as well," said Avigayil. "See you!"

It was a good five-minute walk down the slope from the bungalows to the main area of the Colony. The Brinkman house, flanked by the casino on one side and the *shul* on the other, was a solid white structure from which additions and dormers sprouted like so many afterthoughts. A wide veranda, dotted with assorted porch furniture, snaked around the whole building like a life belt, holding everything together.

Avigayil bounded up the steps, and soon discovered Mrs. Brinkman in her little office to the right of the main entrance. Timidly she knocked at the open door and was greeted immediately with a welcoming smile.

"Well, look who we've got here — Avigayil Kaplan. How nice to see you back! You look great, Avi! You must have grown at least three whole inches, no?"

"Hi!" Avigayil replied, grinning. "I guess I have. How are you? Will the pool be ready this afternoon?"

"Sure. Mr. Brinkman's testing the water this very minute — just one more time. It should be fine, and we'll open for ladies from one to four-thirty, and then the men, same as last year."

Mrs. Brinkman always looked neat and put together, thought Avigayil. Tiny, just an inch or two above a five-foot frame, she exuded efficiency and purpose. She had little time to socialize with the other ladies, making the most of every minute, running, organizing and caring for this community, which was a compact, small world unto itself for more than two months out of the year.

"My mother said you wanted to see me about a job?" asked Avigayil.

"That's right. Grab a chair from over there in the corner, and let's talk."

Mrs. Brinkman pointed to a chart on the wall that showed the bungalows. Next to each was listed the name of the occupants and the number of people in the unit. One cottage remained open.

"Okay," began Mrs. Brinkman. "This is what we have right now. As you can see, most of our regulars are back, *baruch Hashem*, and we also have some newcomers. I've been hatching a plan this winter which I think would be helpful to everyone concerning the orders for kosher groceries: milk, meat, fish, baked goods, etc. The fruit and vegetable truck comes by twice a week, so that's taken care of. But all these years the kosher stuff has been a bit of a hassle, and I think we can get it streamlined, you and I. I thought you could make the rounds twice a week, collect everyone's orders, and then come back down here and phone them through to the stores.

"When we get the deliveries, I'll announce it on the P.A. system and they can come down and collect their stuff. At that time, I'd like you to be right here, to make sure that there's no mix-up. Get it?" Mrs. Brinkman looked straight at Avigayil. "Naturally, I'd pay you. I thought, maybe forty dollars a week, if that's okay?" Now she picked up a red pen and began doodling on an envelope on her desk. "See, I know you don't like working in the day camp, and I figured this might be something you'd enjoy sort of setting up, and," she smiled up at Avigayil, "make a few dollars on the side. What do you say?"

"Sounds okay," said Avigayil, suppressing a smile. 'A few dollars on the side!' If she only knew!

"I could try it for a week or two, and see how it goes. I think people should have their lists ready when I come, though. Otherwise, if they start sitting down to figure out what they need when they see me coming, it'll take all day."

"Smart girl! You're right, and we'll work out all those details. I see your mind's begun spinning already."

Avigayil pushed herself up from the chair, and replaced it in its corner.

"Thanks for thinking of me for this. I'll talk it over with my mother and get back to you. I appreciate it — I really do!" she added.

"You're more than welcome. I just know people will love it, and we'll have a much smoother operation than in the past. Let me know what you decide, okay?" Mrs. Brinkman waved, and turned back to her columns.

Instead of using the well-worn slope uphill to the bungalows, Avigayil decided to circle back the long way. Leaving by the rear door, she skipped down the steps of the veranda and turned left. Sometimes her father came home that way from *shul*, although it took three times as long. He never tired of saying that this walk was the best medicine around, and if you only knew how to breathe slowly and deeply along the pinewood path, it was enough to sustain you all week in the city.

Piney Woods encircled the greater part of the Brinkmans' property, and had given it its name. The woods were part of a National State Park whose entrance was only half a mile down the main road. There were glorious nature trails, a good-sized lake with boats, and numerous picnic areas. All this made the location of Piney Hollow Bungalow Colony very desirable. There was never a problem about filling up the place.

Avigayil followed the footpath along the low wire fence, which marked the boundary between the colony and the woods. This job might not be such a bad thing, she thought. It would give her something to do. Shuli worked in the day camp every day until 4 o'clock, with an hour's lunch break. She griped and complained about the hours, the head counselor, the whiny kids, and the interfering parents, but underneath it all, Avigayil knew she'd be miserable without it. The fact was, Shuli was great with people of all ages. It was a talent, a real gift; probably inherited from their father.

And where Shuli excelled, Avigayil felt herself to be a dismal failure. Sometimes she thought about herself long and hard. She knew she was shy with most adults, and in all new situations. She tended to read aloud in class in a very low voice, barely above a whisper, and teachers had little patience for that. This had been going on since first grade, and perhaps earlier than that! It wasn't that she didn't understand the work; she did very well on tests. So what on earth was it? At home she was completely different, and her Bubby Babsie even favored her over Shuli; she had no idea why, but somehow she knew this to be so.

She wondered whether collecting orders from each bungalow might prove to be too hard after all. Now that she thought about it, what would she do when people started conversations? She'd probably wilt. Of course Mommy would definitely encourage her to go ahead, and she would most likely be right. 'Perhaps it's a chance I should grab!' she thought. 'I'd just have to psyche myself up to be very matter-of-fact and business-like. Like "Hello," she said out loud to herself. "I've come for your order." Or: "Hi! It's me. Have you got your grocery lists ready?" Wow! Was that ever original!

'I'm just not the "original," creative type,' thought Avigayil. 'I can't even come up with a bright idea on how to spend my wonderful inheritance.' As she trudged along, her eyes on the narrow path, she tried to concentrate on her options and, at the same time, to breathe in deeply and exhale vigorously. 'Ta would be proud of me,' she thought, 'but I do wish I could think of something fun and worthwhile while I'm doing all this breathing. Something really different; something spectacular!'

As the path swerved to the left again, bringing her to the far end of the field in back of the bungalows, she noticed a little cabin. She couldn't remember ever having noticed it before. It was built from dark brown logs, weathered now and turned silvery in places, with a slate roof from which several shingles seemed to be missing. The windows on either side of the front door were cracked, and rough boards had been nailed diagonally across to prevent entry.

Avigayil stepped up close to get a better look. Hung from the door at a tipsy angle was a sign. "Pete's Place," she read. "No Trespasing Aloud!" Avigayil giggled. Pete wasn't the world's greatest speller, whoever he was, but that hadn't stopped him from staking out his turf. Shielding her eyes with both hands, she peered inside through the broken glass.

There was one square room, piled high with refuse, broken sticks of furniture, tires, an upended sink, a mattress with coils springing up from its stuffing, pots and dishes, and against one wall, a bicycle minus both wheels. She thought she could make out a door in the far wall, probably the bathroom.

The smell seeping out through the broken glass panes was overpowering. Ugh! She wondered why on earth the Brinkmans hadn't gotten rid of this dump. It was such an eyesore! Judging from the odor, there must have been three generations of skunks holed up in there, or at least a couple of decomposing rats. Phew! No deep breathing around here!

Stepping back onto the path, she gave one last glance at the crooked, filthy shed; staring at the sign, she was lost in wonder. Who was this Pete and when had he lived here? Had she stumbled on some intriguing mystery? Finally she turned and came to the top of the trail and out into what everyone called the Back Field. Strewn liberally with dandelions and plantain, it was nevertheless beloved by all for its sheer size and swaying wild grasses, never mowed but left to its sun-kissed self. Each summer this meadow served up a breathtaking palette of wildflowers, which perked up the greens of the grasses with infinite varieties of color, as if to say: 'Here's my gift to you, for allowing me the freedom to be myself. Walk through my unmarked paths, refresh your tired senses with my floral throw, and bless your Creator for what He has allowed me to offer you.'

Mrs. Kaplan was just gathering up her index cards and putting everything into one enormous manila envelope for further perusal.

"Hi, there! Well, how did it go?"

"Hi, Ma!" Avigayil flopped down onto the grass at her mother's feet, and told her exactly what had been discussed at the main house.

"*Nu*, so how does it sound to you, Avi?" asked her mother.

"I'm not sure," answered Avigayil. "It's easy enough … I'm sure I could set it up and probably get it to run smoothly. Calling in to the stores doesn't bother me, either, because I'm on the phone and I don't have to make small talk; just say what I have to say, being very technical, clear and fast. I can do all that. But…. I'm scared to go to all these bungalows … and you know…."

"Avi, here's what I think: It's a great opportunity for you. You must realize that everyone will understand that it's a job, pure and simple. You're not a visitor they have to entertain. A few words exchanged, maybe something they want to explain about their order, and a friendly wave good-bye. Avi, it's custom-tailored for you! It will force you to interact with a group of very nice people on a regular but not intimate footing, one step at a time. It might lead to your overcoming some of your shyness, it really might. And also, the extra money is nice. Even millionaires always want to have more," smiled Mrs. Kaplan. "Come on in; let's make some lunch. Shuli will be here any minute."

# Chapter Five

The announcement came over the P.A. system that evening: Avigayil Kaplan would pick up written grocery orders between the hours of 9 and 10 A.M. the next morning, and twice weekly, Sundays and Wednesdays, thereafter. Deliveries to the main house, on Mondays and Thursdays, would be announced, and families were asked to please cooperate fully and pick up their orders as soon as possible to prevent spoilage of perishables, for which there were no storage facilities available.

Before she went to sleep, Avigayil, using a copy of Mrs. Brinkman's chart, had mapped out her route and was now lying in her single bed tense and nervous, trying once again to come up with comical one-liners to open up communications. Just before she finally dropped off to sleep, she suddenly landed a beauty. 'Do you remember anyone called Pete who lived in a ramshackle old hut in the far corner of the Back Field? Mrs...Mrs...Mrs...' A sweet smile of relief played around her lips as she began whispering *Kerias Shema*.

Next morning, without having been able to swallow a single bite of breakfast, she set out with grim determination and one order, her mother's, tucked into the small carry-all strapped around her middle. She had decided to begin with the Neufelds, who lived the furthest from their own bungalow.

Already from a good distance away, she was able to make out the two figures at the picnic table, shaded by the clump of birch trees that grew at the periphery of the bungalows. Mrs. Neufeld was probably studying with Esti, Avigayil figured, but at the same time, rocking a stroller back and forth. As she came closer, she heard the familiar words, droned in the tune used in school for *davening*: '*V'ahavta es Hashem Elokecha bechol levavcha ...*' Esti was reciting the *tefillah* slowly and noisily, but she did keep her eyes on her mother's finger, which patiently moved across the page at a snail's pace.

Avigayil simply hated to interrupt, but as soon as Mrs. Neufeld noticed her, she jumped to her feet.

"Finish up to *uvishorecha*, Esti; I'll be right back."

She shoved the stroller handle at Avigayil and with an urgent whisper she implored, "Would you mind rocking him for a second? So sorry, but if I stop now, it'll break the rhythm, and he'll be up all morning," and then, turning to go into the house, she added, "and I really must have that time for Esti. Thanks."

Esti continued her davening without looking up, and Avigayil vigorously rocked the stroller. In a moment Mrs. Neufeld rushed back.

"Here, Avi. I've got it all ready for you. Such a convenience to have you picking up the orders! I've got a million things lined up to do today, and this will be a big help. Okay, here are two sheets, one for the meat and fish, and the rest is all the other stuff. You're an angel! And, by the way, did I tell you how you've grown?" But before Avigayil could reply, or get a word in edgewise, she turned to Esti. "Shsh! Esti, not so loud! I think Moishie's finally sleeping." Without further ado, she wheeled the stroller and parked it a few feet away in the shade, ducked under the laundry line already chock-full of dripping clothes at this time of the morning, and disappeared into the back of the bungalow.

Avigayil glanced over at the little girl, who was now intent on removing a scab from her knee, the *siddur* still open on the table. Somehow, she felt she couldn't just ignore her and walk away. Closing the *siddur* and kissing it, she smiled at the now upturned, freckled face.

"Hi, Esti!" she said.

"I know you ... you're nice," returned Esti. "What's your name?"

"I remember you, too, from last year. My name's Avi Kaplan. I'm sorry, I've got to run. See you later; 'bye!"

She waved and started off on her rounds. That one had been a cinch! There certainly hadn't been time to get all shy and tongue-tied. When you were around Mrs. Neufeld, there was only room for action, no chatting!

Her waist-pack bulging with notes and scraps of paper of every color, shape and size, Avigayil headed for home. She had called at 19 bungalows (one was still vacant), and now, with her mother's list, she had a grand total of 20 orders. It certainly needed organizing, but she was good at that. She settled down at the kitchen table, and slowly, carefully, reviewed everything she had. The more she read, the more she became aware of the need to simplify all of this. She would run off a master sheet and distribute these to each household, order blanks of sorts, with a list of items that people could easily check off, then add any extra items on the bottom of the page. A large loose-leaf binder would be a great help for filing the orders and keeping things neat. As for today, she'd just have to manage with what she had.

Down in the main house, Mrs. Brinkman was ready for her with the names and telephone numbers of the kosher suppliers. She cleared a corner of her desk, which as usual was piled high with folders, leaflets, correspondence, and today a brand-new bathroom plunger, laid atop everything else as if it were a paperweight.

"Excuse the somewhat bizarre décor in here right now. Believe me, there's a method to this madness in spite of what you think," she told Avigayil with a smile. "Look, here's a cordless phone for you, and you can go right ahead. Will you be okay?"

"Fine," Avigayil nodded, trying to hide the nervous jitters that played havoc with her insides. She pulled out the orders and laid them on the desk with what she hoped seemed like superb efficiency.

"Wow," gasped Mrs. Brinkman. "I bet some of these were barely legible. Any questions before you begin?"

Avigayil explained how she planned to draft order blanks and asked for the use of the copy machine.

"Excellent idea! Of course that's the way to go, only I hadn't thought of it. Great! I knew I'd picked a winner." She gave Avigayil a friendly pat on the back. "I'll leave you to it now and go to the rescue of the flood victims in... oh, never mind, mustn't gossip; wherever the blessed thing's stopped up!" With a mischievous grin, she sailed out of the room, bearing the plunger aloft like a baton.

The job took quite a while and became easier as she went along. By the time she was up to number sixteen, Avigayil felt a rush of adrenalin and the confidence that came with it. Why, this was going to be fun!

Later, at lunch, Avigayil thought she detected a glimmer of amusement in her mother's eyes as she and Shuli compared notes on their morning's activities. Shuli had organized a major treasure hunt.

"The hardest thing to find was a LIVE something; humans excluded," she told them, taking a huge bite out of her tuna sandwich.

"Ugh!" interjected Avigayil, thinking of the hordes of creepy-crawlies that had to be making their home in 'Pete's Place.' That hovel would have been a gold mine for those treasure hunters.

"Anyhow, the thing got totally out of hand," Shuli continued. "Pessie Green and the Gordon kid found the same ant, in the same split second, and they started fighting and clawing each other for the legal rights. In the end, the ant was delivered to the judges dead as a doornail, squashed flat by the two warring teams. Finally we had to trash it due to its lack of vital signs." She giggled and took a long drink of ice water. "How did your morning go, Avi?" she asked. "How does a wealthy kid like you feel, working for a living like the rest of us?"

Avigayil was surprised that there was, in fact, plenty to tell, and in the telling, she realized she'd had an interesting, satisfying and even enjoyable experience.

"Of course, the second part of this may turn out to be the hardest," she wondered aloud. "The stores will make mistakes and deliver stuff that wasn't ordered, or they'll try to substitute things for whatever they're out of. Oh, well. Mrs. Brinkman will just have to bail me out if things get too rough. Right, Ma?"

Mrs. Kaplan, sipping her coffee, nodded.

"Of course she will," she said. "It'll take a while, but soon it will all straighten out and become routine. I just know you can handle it like a pro, Avi."

She leaned back and smiled at the girls. "I think it's going to turn out to be a great summer this year. I'll leave you both to clean up and I'll catch a nap, okay? I can't wait to get into the pool later; isn't this the most gorgeous weather?"

Later that evening a car pulled up in front of the vacant unit, and as the old-timers surreptitiously watched, a father, mother and a boy of about eight or nine carried their belongings into the bungalow. Mrs. Kaplan was one of the first brave souls to break the ice. With a big smile of welcome, she walked over and offered food or anything else the newcomers might need. The 'Pineys' in general were a friendly, outgoing crowd, and fruit, cookies, etc., soon filled the counters in the little kitchen area.

At supper, Mrs. Kaplan reported to the girls that the Lowingers were already well settled in.

"That child is definitely a *ben zekunim*," she said. "The parents must be well into their fifties, and I gather that their main reason for coming here is for the benefit of this child. His mother said that she could never bring herself to send him to a sleep-away camp, and they'd been told about our great day camp here. There's nothing for him in the city, so she has high hopes for Piney Hollow."

"I did notice him standing around, casing the joint," said Shuli. "Why is he wearing Shabbos clothes — a white shirt and tie — on a moving-in-trip to a bungalow colony, for goodness' sake?"

"Who knows?" answered Mrs. Kaplan. "His name's Nesanel, by the way, and I just hope they found the right place for him. It's obviously a major concern with them."

The phone rang; it was Mr. Kaplan, making his nightly check-in call.

"Wanna come along for Scrabble?" asked Shuli.

"Not really, thanks," said Avigayil. "Where are you playing tonight?"

"At the Gordons. What is it with you? Why don't you come, too? We could easily find eight kids to play two boards."

Avigayil shrugged. The truth was, she had no idea why she preferred to be alone so often. It was just so, and she saw no reason to fight it. It was so much simpler all around, and contrary to what everyone must think, she was never lonely.

"See ya!" Shuli was out the door and running along the path.

Avigayil decided to relax on the glider that, amongst a goodly assortment of gradually acquired outdoor equipment, graced their screened-in porch. Through the half-open door, she heard her mother telling her father about their able older daughter and her new enterprise. Avigayil grinned. Mommy couldn't conceal her secret hope that this venture would miraculously 'bring her out of her shell.' It was a lost cause to try to convince her parents that she was very cozy in that shell.

She settled back into the cushions, and slowly her eyes became accustomed to the dark. The evening sounds of the colony filtered pleasantly through her thoughts: a mother calling to her children to come in from play, screen doors slamming, and intermittent bursts of laughter from the Scrabble players a few doors down. On the porch next door, Zeidy Breich was listening to a taped lecture. It was not intrusive like some of those music tapes that you only wanted to hear when YOU had them playing. This was definitely a *shiur* of some kind, but you could not actually hear the words.

Suddenly, she was aware of soft steps on the grass outside, followed by a timid knock on the door.

Avigayil jumped up, the glider letting out a rusty squeak in shock.

"Hi, there!" she called. "You're a Neufeld, right?" She smiled at the boy who was clutching Esti's hand tightly. "What a nice surprise! Come on in. Hello, Esti! Out so late at night?"

Esti's face was radiant. Then, suddenly overcome by her own daring, she buried her head in the crook of her brother's arm.

"What's your name?" Avigayil asked the boy.

"Yanky," he said. "Esti's been begging my mother to let her come and see you. Finally my mother gave in and said okay, but just for ten minutes — not more! So, I had to walk her down here. Is that all right?" This was obviously not a job that he relished.

"Sure, it's great! I've been sitting here waiting for a friend. It's perfect! You know what, Yanky? You go on home, and I'll bring her back soon. Tell your mother it's fine and not to worry," said Avigayil.

"Thanks," muttered Yanky gratefully, and he was gone in a flash, relieved to be rid of his embarrassing mission so painlessly.

Avigayil put her arm around the little girl's shoulder.

"Come and sit with me on the glider," she told her, "and we'll do some rocking."

She took the child's hand in hers and settled her on the seat at her side. "Back and forth," she said. "Back and forth."

"Back and fore," echoed Esti with enthusiasm. "Back and fore."

"Do you have a glider on your porch?"

Esti shook her head, in the negative.

"It's fun, right?"

"Uh-huh," agreed Esti, rocking as hard as she was able.

"What did you have for supper?" asked Avigayil.

Esti had to think about that one.

"Macaroni and cheese?" she asked doubtfully. She sounded as if she was afraid she'd given the wrong answer to a question in school.

"Are you asking me? I don't know what you had. I wasn't in your house tonight," said Avigayil very matter-of-factly. "Still, it sounds good. I bet you did have macaroni and cheese. We had corn on the cob. Do you like corn?"

"Uh-huh," replied Esti, with great emphasis, rocking some more.

"Did Shuli take you kids swimming today?" asked Avigayil.

"I just went in to my ankles," said Esti. "Shuli's your sister?"

"Yep. How many sisters do you have? I just have Shuli."

"I have about four?" Again, Esti looked worried.

"You go home and count tonight, and tell me tomorrow, okay? And now, d'you want to go back?"

"Uh-uh." Esti liked it here. She was definitely the most important person on this glider.

"You know, Mommy will get worried if you stay too long. I'll show you some fireflies on the way home. Let's go!"

"Flies with fire?" Esti wasn't about to move for a bunch of flies.

"Fireflies," said Avigayil, firmly, but making the words sound like the ultimate adventure. "Come on, pal!"

# *Chapter Six*

The boxes, clearly marked with names, were lined up along the wall on the Brinkmans' back porch. Avigayil, pad in hand, carefully checked each delivery against her own list, to make sure that none had been omitted. They all seemed to be accounted for. Through the open door, she nodded at Mrs. Brinkman, on the phone at her desk, and circled her thumb and index finger signaling: A-Okay! She wasn't quite as confident as this gesture meant to convey to her 'boss.' In fact, she was apprehensive and nervous. She wished the boxes already magically whisked away in a single swoop. There'd be no such luck. And since this was the very first 'pick-up,' she knew she had to stay on the job and see it through.

The announcement had been made, and sure enough, here they came! People rushed in, straggled in, and even jogged down the slope. They were armed with the weirdest assortment of equipment. Bags of all colors and materials, strollers with and without babies, red toy wagons, and one or two even brought shopping carts 'borrowed' from unidentified super markets. Several of them would have to make two trips, and others were lugging a double load, one for themselves and one for their neighbor. And then, quite incredibly, in less than one hour, the entire event was over.

"Phew!" Avigayil stared at the now-empty space against the wall. 'One down and how many to go?' she thought to herself.

She left the porch and approached Mrs. Brinkman, who asked, "Well, that went very well, didn't it?"

"I'm surprised they all turned up in such a hurry," she answered. "By the way, how do they pay?"

"Oh, the bills are included in the orders, and customers pay by mail, or they drop into the stores when they're in Monticello," said Mrs. Brinkman. "Wanna show me?" she added, pointing to the flyers Avigayil carried.

Shyly, Avigail handed over a sheaf of neatly typed pink sheets, clearly divided into columns, over which she'd been laboring all morning before the deliveries had arrived.

"I'll give each family a whole batch of them today, and they can fill them out as they go along," she said.

"Great!" exclaimed Mrs. Brinkman, scanning the list. "I see you're right on top of it: whole milk, skim milk and 99%, too. Fabulous! Incidentally, when's your mother starting at camp this year?"

"Some time next week. They don't begin with big productions until they've settled in. 'Bye now; see you! And thanks for the job," she managed to add. Retrieving her stack of lists, she skipped down the back steps and was on her way.

Once again she elected to go back along the woods. There was something elusive pulling her towards that deserted shack. Somehow it had opened up all sorts of exciting possibilities to her imagination.

The sun was strong and the aroma of acres of pine trees drenched the air. A rabbit scurried out from under the fence on her right and dashed across her path before she had a chance to get a good look. Avigayil shaded her eyes and squinted hard to discover where it was hiding in the tall grass. There was absolutely no trail, nothing to reveal that somewhere, perhaps a foot or two away, a creature with quivering whiskers and a puffy white tail was lying low and watching her with two wary eyes!

She marched on, and once again the little house became the focus of her attention. What if she got inside somehow? What if she looked around? What if it wasn't that bad after all? What if she got her hands on it? What if...

She kept her eyes on the path ahead, her mind racing, her pace quickening, and arriving at the turn she looked up. There it was!

Avigayil placed her batch of papers on the grass and weighed them down with a smooth rock. With her back to the shed, she surveyed the immediate surroundings. The meadow, wide and rich, lay in the noon sun, pulsing with the life of small creatures, bright wild flowers, and a soft breeze playing with the tops of the grasses. Butterflies fluttered from one blossom to another; bees followed suit, paying their visits and staying for just seconds, and high above, birds sailed, swooped and flew ... wherever. She had no idea where birds flew, unless perhaps to feed their young — or maybe just for exercise. Ta would approve of that! She smiled, and turned on her heel to gaze once more at Pete's home.

The old rusty padlock contraption held. It would certainly

refuse to be tampered with. Wooden boards were nailed across the broken windows, like giant multiplication signs. They left gaps and jagged edges through which Avigayil peered, bending over, but steering clear so as not to cut her hands.

Giving her imagination full range, she stared at what there was, and dreamed at what perhaps there might be. Was there really a bathroom at the back? Slowly, she circled the hut, and found a worn narrow stretch of grass between the woods and the building. A small glazed window set high up remained unbroken, and mirrored the sunlight. Looking in from the front, no such light had been visible. This must be the other room, probably a tiny bathroom, she figured.

As for the main area, once it was rid of all that junk, it would be a good size, much like their bedroom at home, she thought.

Suddenly, something struck her with a stab of doubt. She remembered the missing shingles. Did the roof leak? Through the windows she studied the floor intently, at least those parts that were not strewn with garbage. With a sigh of relief she noted that nothing seemed wet or rotted.

She looked up once more at the slanty roof, and saluted with a grateful wink.

There was so much to think about! In her mind, she conjured up the image of an elderly lady, sitting at a window high above the rooftops of a village in South Africa, writing a letter to her. "Doreen," she whispered, "what do you think?"

Picking up her lists, she decided to time the walking distance between here and their bungalow. Filled with enormous excitement and a new rush of energy, she started out. It was three minutes from door to door, and in those few moments, the flimsy stirrings hidden deep inside her for the past two days emerged into the sunlight. The first beginnings of an amazing plan had been born.

# Chapter Seven

During Thursday night it rained without letup, but by morning the sun was out again, and all was well with the world.

"You'll have to move over into the bunk bed for Shabbos, Avi," said Mrs. Kaplan. "Tatty's bringing Bubby out. Here's some clean linen; you can make up the bed for her."

"Oh, great!" said Avigayil. "Is she staying the week?"

"No. Not till August. That's when she likes to take her two weeks. Remember last year? Tatty'll take her back with him on Sunday night." She stepped over to the refrigerator and viewed its contents with a practiced eye. "Okay, let's see — fish first."

And soon the *erev Shabbos* aroma began to waft through the close quarters of the bungalow.

Avigayil changed the beds and gave their room a good going-over. It would have been much nicer for Bubby to have her privacy, but this was life in the country, and the very few three-bedroom units here were reserved for larger families. Bubby didn't really mind. "You've got to be a good sport," she'd say, using one of her typically English expressions. "Always make the best of every situation." Avigayil surveyed her handiwork and found it adequate. Was there anything else?

"Ma, I'm going to get some Shabbos flowers," she called over her shoulder on her way to the back field. She chose some grasses and tall, slender flowers for the table, and a small, colorful bouquet for Bubby's windowsill. Sweet peas, Doreen had written, or pansies. These had been Abby Silver's delight and joy. Well, thought Avigayil, in Piney Hollow it would have to be blue chicory, which grew wild and tall in abundance at the roadsides and in the meadow. There were daisies galore, white Queen Anne's lace, flat and round as paper doilies, and a few sturdy buttercups for color.

She'd have to create an opportunity to get Bubby all to herself and then share her secret. Today would be one more day that she could hug it, think about it, toy with it, and treasure it without anyone in the whole world even suspecting a thing. After that, if Bubby approved, this wisp of an idea would gather momentum — others would have to become part of it, and eventually it might develop into a reality instead of a private, exciting dream.

After arranging her flowers, she helped her mother peel the vegetables, and then made her favorite ice cream. It was the lull before the storm for Mrs. Kaplan. This Sunday, she would be meeting with the head of Drama at nearby Camp Zimra, to discuss the costumes for their major play and all the other odds and ends that needed her expertise. The job of designing and super-vising all the work in that department had been hers for years. It was well paid, she loved doing it, and this was the main rea-son they still came to Piney Hollow.

"Did your Bais Yaakov ever put on something called 'Shefford'? I think that's what they're planning at Zimra. It's about Jewish children in England during the war." asked Mrs. Kaplan.

"No," answered Avigayil. "But I know they had a play about that in Montreal. It was supposed to be fabulous! You know, that's something Bubby would really be able to help you with. She'd remember what kids wore then and all that."

"She might," replied her mother thoughtfully. "It's an amaz-ing story. All children, Jewish and non-Jewish, were whisked out of London in the nick of time. I think it was on a Friday, two days before the war was declared. The called it Evacuation, and it meant that kids would be out of harm's way during the bombing.

"Thousands and thousands of children were placed in villages all over England for the duration of the war. And of course for Jewish kids that was an experience none of them will ever forget. They lived with gentiles and kept all the mitzvos. I think some of them were evacuated for close to five years. Imagine that? You're absolutely right about Bubby. Maybe she was even there!"

They worked on, side by side, while the music of the latest *Tzlil V'zemer* tape filled the room. The idea of Bubby's possi-ble input fired Mrs. Kaplan with excitement.

Neither of them heard the timid knock on the door, and were totally surprised to suddenly find Esti in their kitchen.

"Well, look who's here!" announced Avigayil. "Good morn-ing, Esti Neufeld, and how are you doing?"

Esti crept up to Mrs. Kaplan and watched intently as the chicken quarters were expertly spiced and coated. Avigayil noticed that she was tightly clutching some papers in one hand, behind her back.

"Hi, Esti," said Mrs. Kaplan, handing her the box of cornflake crumbs. "Give a shake, go ahead! But not too much; watch it!"

Esti stood stock-still. Then she shook her head silently.

"What's wrong?" asked Mrs. Kaplan. "You can do it — it's easy! We'll do it together. I'll hold the box with you, okay?"

Esti looked over at Avigayil as if seeking her opinion.

"Go ahead," encouraged Avigayil. "It's fun!"

Esti reluctantly held the corner of the box, while Mrs. Kaplan did the actual job. It was obvious that the little girl was terrified of ruining something.

This morning she looked adorable. Her hair was done up in two thin pigtails that sprouted from her head like miniature fountains. Her glasses perched on her little upturned nose gave her a distinctly studious look. She wore a red t-shirt and blue denim skirt with red stitching and buttons. 'Her mother tries so hard,' Avigayil thought, 'but it's not working. Something just seems to be blocking Esti's road to progress and success. Maybe she really hasn't got what it takes to be a model student, or even a mediocre one. But then again, perhaps there's a magic key to unlock some abilities that she does have and isn't using.'

"Fine," said Mrs. Kaplan, opening the oven. "It's hot already. In you go!" She addressed the tray of cutlets, as she slid them smoothly into place and closed the door. "And now, we can clean up this mess," she added with an exaggerated sigh.

"What are those papers?" Avigayil asked Esti. "I mean the ones behind your back!" she smiled.

Esti did not immediately oblige. Instead of answering, she turned on her heel, ran outside to the porch, plopped herself upon the glider and began to rock. By the time Avigayil joined her, her hands were empty.

"D'you want me to guess where those papers are?" Avigayil asked.

Esti grinned, then giggled and nodded.

Avigayil decided to play this for all it was worth. She made an elaborate game of searching every nook and cranny — under the chairs, up on the ledges — no papers!

"Okay. Open your mouth wide, and let's see whether you swallowed them and there are some pieces stuck between your teeth," she said.

Esti found this hilarious, and opened up wide while Avigayil peered inside with utmost concentration. At that moment, Esti jumped up, almost knocking Avigayil sideways, and at the same time, triumphantly held up the sheets of paper on which, of course, she'd been sitting all this time.

"Brilliant!" declared Avigayil. "So now let's see them."

It was Esti's summer homework; there was one sheet for Hebrew and one for English and math.

"Oh, so you're supposed to do these for school, right? Do you need help?"

Esti nodded.

"Why me?" asked Avigayil.

Esti shrugged her shoulders, then dug deep into her skirt pocket and produced a bedraggled piece of paper. She handed it to Avigayil, studying her covertly while the older girl smoothed out the crumpled note and read.

> Dear Avi,
> It's Erev Shabbos, and Moishie's very cranky. He has a bit of temperature. I'm sending this S.O.S. HELP! Can you spare a little time to do these sheets with Esti? It's important she doesn't miss a day, and I'm absolutely snowed under. Appreciate much! But only if your mother can spare you.
> Gratefully, Mrs. Neufeld

'It's funny,' Avigayil thought, 'but it must be a sign from

Hashem. It's pointing me exactly down the road I'm heading for.' She looked at the little girl who was watching her intently, sucking her thumb while scratching her leg with the other hand.

"Well, Esti, Mommy says it's okay if I do your work with you today, so let's go out to the back. The picnic table's the best place. But first, we need a magic pointer; let's see if we can find one."

'Now where did that crazy idea spring from? she wondered. But at least it produced immediate results. Esti clapped her hands and, pigtails bobbing, followed her without a moment's hesitation. After rejecting several sticks of various lengths and thicknesses, bare or endowed with sprouts and leaves, they finally settled on a clean, neat piece of a branch, which was hardly longer than a regular pencil. Avigayil disappeared into the house, stealing a quick look at the kitchen clock. Tatty usually got in by about four. There was plenty of time; it was only twelve-thirty now. Searching in the kitchen drawer, she found what she wanted and rejoined Esti holding a sharp knife. It didn't take her long to whittle a fairly satisfactory point.

"Perfect!" she said, admiring her own handiwork. "Here, it's for you to use. Let's start with the Hebrew sheet. Point and read!" she ordered.

The Hebrew homework consisted of two-letter words with vowels. These were boldly and clearly printed in large type. There were a total of fifteen words, in three lines of five each.

It was slow, painstaking work, but Avigayil found that with patience and warmth she could make things happen. The pointer worked its magic.

"Can I keep it?" asked Esti when they were done.

"Of course," Avigayil told her. "We'll have a little break now, and make a different one for the English homework. Okay?"

Ten minutes later, equipped with pointer number two, they set to work on the second assignment. Here an adult was required to read a brief paragraph to Esti, and then ask her five questions relating to the contents. Esti did not seem to have difficulty with this. She answered quickly and correctly. Avigayil decided to venture a little further, and add her own questions that probed somewhat deeper, searching for cause and effect rather than the obvious facts. This time Esti lost some of her interest and focus. She was unaccustomed to this line of questioning.

"Now grab that pointer and let's do the reading," instructed Avigayil. There were five words with the short vowel sound of 'a,' all of which occurred in the story. "Excellent! That was a cinch! You're a champion!" said Avigayil. "And you can keep both pointers. Remember, they're magic helpers. Tell your mother you were great! Let's do that again sometime. What do you say? And now, let's see; can you count for me from 1 to 15?"

Esti nodded enthusiastically, and complied amid much swallowing and nodding.

"Very good! Now next time, bring along some little stones. Five or ten pretty, colorful ones. Can you find some around your bungalow?"

"Stones? What for?" asked Esti.

"Wait and see," said Avigayil, investing the words with deep mystery.

"Oh!" cried Esti.

Avigayil got up and scribbled a note to Mrs. Neufeld.

"For your mother," she told Esti, and waved her good-bye. "Good Shabbos, see you," she called, and collided with Shuli as they entered the cottage at the exact same time.

# *Chapter Eight*

**S**habbos was wonderful. At Piney Hollow, Mr. Kaplan traditionally led the *davening* for *Kaballas Shabbos* on Friday nights, and again for *Mussaf* in the mornings. Bubby wouldn't have missed going to *shul* for the world. The girls always joined her, while Mrs. Kaplan slept a little longer and *davened* at home. Bubby was interested in every little thing about their comings and goings. Shuli had to report on her day-camp activities, and for a change, Avigayil had her own job to tell about.

"I collect the orders Sundays and Wednesdays, and the deliveries come in Mondays and Thursdays. What with phoning in to the stores and having to be around for the pick-ups, it takes quite a bit of time. But it's okay and after a while I think I can find ways to make it more efficient."

Bubby was fascinated.

"By the way, who's that child I see lurking about every corner, and always by himself?" she asked on Shabbos afternoon, from her beach chair where she had a grand view of the entire property.

Nesanel Lowinger had just appeared twenty feet away, out of nowhere, and was surveying the small family group through slitted eyes.

"An unnerving little person," she added.

"Now that you put it that way, I guess I would have to agree," said Mrs. Kaplan. "He's an only child of middle-aged parents, and there seem to be problems. They've never been here before, but they heard of our excellent day camp and they desperately hoped he'd fit in — but he hasn't. The kids are ruthless. They didn't accept him from day one — I have no idea why — and they made life so miserable for him that he refuses to go back. The Lowingers booked the cottage for two months, so they're staying, but the mother is in a real state about those kids and the counselors."

"Does he do all right in school during the year?" asked Bubby. "It's not really nice to talk about people, but in this case I suspect help may be needed, and even welcomed."

"I don't like to seem to pry, but I get the feeling that there are definitely difficulties. He must be bright enough — his mother says his marks are very good — but he can't make it socially, I guess," said Mrs. Kaplan, watching the boy who stood rooted to the spot, still as a statue, and yet as if poised to sprint.

"Maybe he's a loner by choice," mused Avigayil.

"There are loners and outcasts," said Bubby, "and outcasts are not where they are by choice!"

Avigayil sighed.

Two other boys, one of them Yanky Neufeld, walked down the path carrying their *sefarim* for the father-son learning groups in the casino. Nesanel, quick as a wink, bent to pick up a pebble and shot it over their heads, aimed perfectly to land at their feet.

"Hey, where did *that* come from?" yelled Yanky. "Crazy!" But, looking behind them, they saw the peaceful group in front of the Kaplans' bungalow — and the retreating back of Nesanel slinking around the corner.

"*Rasha!*" shouted Yanky, brandishing his fist, and then, turning, he began running down the slope, followed by his friend.

"Well, there you are," said Bubby. "Life at Piney Hollow will be interesting this summer. I need a good cup of tea; any volunteers?"

After *Havdalah*, Avigayil managed to corner her grandmother for a moment.

"Bubby, I need an hour all alone with you. Would tomorrow be all right, after I call in the orders? How about eleven or so; could we make a date?"

"How exciting!" cried Bubby. "Curious George isn't a patch on Curious Me! I don't suppose you'd give me a hint as to what this is all about?"

"Doreen," replied Avigayil, "and Pete," she added for good measure.

"Oh!" said Bubby. "And where do we spend this hour?"

"I've thought about that," said Avigayil. "Would it be too much to ask you to meet me at eleven, down at the main house? We could take a walk from there, and have total privacy."

"Done!" Bubby answered cheerfully. "I'll be there, *b'ezras Hashem*. Can't wait!"

Sunday morning Avigayil awoke so early she saw the sky still dusky blue from the long night. She lay very still, trying hard to go back to sleep. But all her senses were sharp and alert and her mind immediately began to race, darting this way and that, in an effort to plan her strategy. Today was the day — and she felt just great! She was up, washed, and *davening* before anyone had even stirred. She set out early on her rounds, beginning, as always, at the Neufelds.

This time Esti was nowhere to be seen. Probably sleeping late, thought Avigayil. Not so her mother! Mrs. Neufeld was already pegging up her laundry on the long, patient line in the back of the house. She was also ready for Avigayil with her food orders.

Her plan worked wonders. People had used the pink order-sheets and, for the most part, there were no delays or waiting around. At the Lowingers, however, there was a problem. Nesanel — she was positive it was he — refused to open the door.

"If you don't open up, Nesanel, you'll have to bring your mother's order down yourself. And I mean it!" She had raised her voice to make sure he heard her. "I'm counting. One — two — and, listen up, three!" She turned on her heel and resolutely strode on to the next bungalow, only to be stopped in her tracks by a distraught Mrs. Lowinger running after her, model's coat flapping, waving the pink sheet of paper.

"Sorry! Nesanel had trouble with the lock. It gets stuck all the time. Here's my order. Adina, dear, — or is it Ahuvah? Just make sure they send the lebens and NOT the yogurts. Thanks so much!" She handed the order to Avigayil with trembling hands.

"I'm Avi; Avigayil Kaplan," she smiled. "No problem! I'll make certain you get exactly what you ordered, don't worry." She waved and quickly fled, thinking: 'This is how her day begins, and no doubt continues, until her head finally hits the pillow at night — what a brat!'

Her calls to the stores were all completed before eleven, and as she stood looking through the window, watching her grandmother coming down the hill, she found herself mumbling a silent prayer.

"'Bye, Mrs. Brinkman," she called in the direction of the office. "All done!" and she left the building.

"Bubby!" she called. "Thanks so much for coming all the way down for me. Was the walk okay?"

"Sure! It's such a gorgeous day, and I'm about to be let in on a secret. What could be better?"

"Then come with me," said Avigayil, and started on the now familiar woodside path. "This is one of Tatty's favorite walks here. You're supposed to breathe in deeply, and exhale noisily. That way, the pine magic enters your system and eventually you become like the Green Giant!"

Avigayil realized she was jabbering away from sheer nervousness.

"So let's do that," said Bubby. "I've always wanted to look like the Green Giant." She marched on, inhaling and sniffing mightily.

'She's giving me time and space — wonderful!' thought Avigayil.

"Close your eyes now," she instructed as they approached the bend. "I'll lead you and tell you when to look." She hooked her grandmother's arm into her own, and continued up the trail.

"Stop!" she commanded. "Open your eyes!" And, with an introductory sweep of her arm, she intoned, "Pete's Place."

The sun shone full on the old shack.

Bubby stared at the hovel and then at her grandchild. Avigayil was watching her with her heart in her eyes, silent.

"Doreen?" Bubby whispered. "Pete?" she added as she stepped closer to read the crooked sign.

Avigayil nodded, spreading her arms wide in a helpless plea.

'Can you see?' she seemed to be saying. 'Can you feel it,

too? You, who have always understood me so well? Can you cut through the trappings and envision the "might-bes" as I have?'

Bubby peered through the windows and then, slowly, circled the house. Avigayil followed without uttering a sound.

"It's a grand little place," was Bubby's verdict at last. "You'll get it to look lovely!"

"Oh, Bubby!" Avigayil gave her grandmother a violent hug, very nearly upsetting the older woman's balance. She was almost in tears. "You're the best in the world — there's nobody like you" She choked on the words.

"Thanks for the compliment!" said Bubby. "And now let's talk."

They found a low flat boulder nearby, on which to do just that.

"I've simply got to have it," Avigayil declared. She picked a long blade of grass, pulling it up gently and carefully, so as to bring up the juicy root she loved to suck.

"I've just plain fallen in love with the idea of creating a place, all my own, and of course fixing it up would be half the fun. Imagine my own world up here! Hardly anyone ever bothers to come all this way. Look at that wild meadow — could anything be more beautiful?" She sucked on her stem and plucked another.

"The whole thing grew inside me, slowly. But I was caught up in it right from the first time I set eyes on the place. Do you know what I mean? And then, everything just sort of fit in. It was really weird. Remember that little kid from our other summers here, Esti Neufeld? Well, she's about six years old now and has finished Pre-1A. The school doesn't want to promote her to first grade."

Bubby, eyes on the cabin, listened intently.

"Sure I remember her. Dear little thing, she is. But I knew she wasn't doing well in school even then."

"I think Hashem kind of sent me a sign," Avigayil continued.

"She keeps coming to me and follows me around. Her mother needs help. Esti's summer homework for each day is a huge burden for her, and she'd be thrilled if I took over. I was thinking that once I got the place fixed up, or even while I'm doing it, I'd take her up here and work with her, play with her, and you know, try to build up her self-esteem. She's quite pitiful, always thinking that whatever she'll answer is going to be wrong. My mind's just bursting with ideas!"

"I think I get the general drift," said Bubby. And then she added, "Tell me, have you spoken to your parents or Shuli about this?"

"No, not yet. Remember what Doreen wrote: 'When you decide what to do with the money, go for it! Do exactly what you want, but check it out with Bubby Babsie first. She'd know whether it would make our mother proud and happy.' "

"Okay, so let's brainstorm awhile and look at the different angles," said Bubby. "It's probably a much bigger project than you picture in your mind right now. The place is a wreck! Also, I haven't the faintest idea of what the Brinkmans will say, or what costs would be entailed. But, having said all that, I adore the idea, and certainly the Esti angle adds the beauty of a very big *mitzvah* to the whole thing.

"As for our mother, there's not a shred of doubt in my mind that she would have been delighted. A little nervous, perhaps, at so much money being spent; remember, she never had enough for the barest essentials. Still, all this," and she swept her arm over the rich display of summer's bounty, "would have brought her immense joy, as obviously it does to you. Chip off the old block, that's what you are."

"Can I afford it, do you think?"

"Before we get all flustered about this, I suggest we talk to the others, and then explore the loathsome technicalities. Unfortunately, the most wondrous of dreams are usually fraught with down-to-earth, annoying details and limitations. A great deal will depend upon the Brinkmans."

"I know," said Avigayil. "Tatty will have to do some wheeling and dealing over there, I'm sure. Oh, Bubby! If it works out, it will be all ready and in operation by the time you come for your vacation. By the way, do *you* remember Pete?"

"No, not even this cabin. I've never really seen it; do you know that? It took *you* to do that! I'm proud of you!" She got up, brushed herself off, and they started toward the bungalow.

'Funny,' thought Avigayil, 'back until half an hour ago, my secret filled me up completely, ... it was like holding my breath under water until I'm almost bursting with the pressure of it! But now that I've shared it, somehow it hasn't become less; on the contrary! Maybe that's because now it's more real. How does that saying go? "Sorrow shared is half the sorrow, happiness shared, is double the joy."'

She was so excited! But she must try to temper her eagerness with reason. There were many ifs and buts. The Brinkmans, of course, were a huge question mark. She herself wasn't completely sure of what all the answers would be. Should she really sink everything into what would basically always be a summer project?

"Make sure you bring Esti over before we leave this evening," Bubby said just before they reached the bungalow. "But whether 'Pete's Place' happens or not — and you know that I hope, for your sake, with all my heart that it does — I'm certain you can make a difference with that child, whichever route you'll go."

# Chapter Nine

L unch on Sundays in the country was always *fleishig,* most of it leftovers from Shabbos. That way, Mr. Kaplan never had to worry about supper when he got home. Usually he took along a sandwich, some fruit and maybe a Danish. It was a good arrangement.

Avigayil and Bubby had decided that the 'proclamation' should be made in grand style, right after the soup. Avigayil, knees shaking, got up and collected the plates and spoons. She deposited them on the counter, and then, leaning back against the sink, her arms tightly folded for extra courage, she announced dramatically:

"Hear ye, hear ye, hear ye! A momentous decision has been

made! It's about the money!" At this point, she hiccuped and swallowed for air. All eyes were upon her, but by positioning herself a few feet away, and standing while they sat, it was truly as if she were addressing them almost formally.

"I've kind of decided what I want to do with it." There, it was out!

Bubby gave her a thumbs-up and a wink.

"You have?" said Mr. Kaplan. "At long last? Well, that's great! Tell us all about it, but Avi, can you bring us the second course and we can eat while we listen? Go on, Shuli, help your sister get the show on the road. I'm sure Mommy and Bubby can't wait to hear; as for me, I'm starving, and I think we can do both together, eat as well as absorb what you have to tell us."

Avi couldn't help but smile. Trust her father to have his priorities straight!

"Tell me! Tell me!" Shuli hissed as they dished out the chicken and *kugel*. "Why haven't you said a word to me? What is it? We're really going to *Eretz Yisrael*, right?" She gave Avigayil a friendly shove while bearing the steaming *cholent*.

Avigayil carried assorted salad remnants and found space for them on the small crowded table.

"So sorry, Shuli; no, it's nothing like that," she said. And then, turning to her parents, she continued: "Bubby already knows all about it. Remember? That was Doreen's wish. So I showed her this morning."

Bubby looked positively smug.

"Well, I must say that was a very nice gesture on Doreen's part, and yes, I'm already in on this. Still, I'm going to leave it to Avi to explain."

"What do you mean, you 'showed' it to Bubby? Have you bought something we don't even know about?" asked Mrs. Kaplan.

"No, but it's something I want to buy; maybe, that is."

Avigayil decided to plunge ahead while the others ate and stared at her. She couldn't swallow a bite anyhow.

"It's a little cabin on the grounds here; right at the edge of the back field where it meets the path alongside Piney Woods."

"A cabin? Are you crazy or something?" Shuli burst forth. "What kind of cabin?"

"Listen, and I'll tell you," said Avigayil. Her face was flushed and her dark brown eyes sparkled with excitement, as the words tumbled out.

"It's an old neglected hut, or unit, if you like, where a guy called Pete once lived. Maybe he was the handyman around here before the Brinkmans bought this place. It's locked and boarded up, so I haven't been inside, but it looks okay through the windows. Listen," she said, begging the unbelieving audience to give her the benefit of their doubt, "it's filthy, and piled high with garbage. But it's sound and solid in the walls and roof. At least that's what I'm banking on. It's a perfect spot for what I want."

"Go on," encouraged Mr. Kaplan, chewing with gusto.

"I want it. I want to make it my own. I want to clean it up, fix it up, and then use it. My idea is to have a kind of retreat, like a secret clubhouse or tree house that kids have. I want it to be my own hide-away, and if it all works out, maybe I can do something even more fabulous with it."

"Like what?" Mommy had stopped eating, and propped her elbow on the table. She leaned her chin into the palm of her hand and regarded her daughter with rapt attention.

"Well, I thought I'd take Esti Neufeld up there to tutor her; do her summer homework with her ... you know?" she finished lamely.

"Are you serious, Avi?" Shuli couldn't contain herself any longer. "After giving *maaser*, you have 4,500 bucks, and you're gonna blow it on Esti Neufeld?" She sounded flabbergasted.

"Hold it, everybody. Let's not go overboard here. First of all, does anyone know whether the Brinkmans would be willing to sell?" asked Mr. Kaplan. "And if so, for how much?"

"Not yet," said Avigayil. "We were sort of hoping, that is, Bubby and I, that that's where you'd come in! What do *you* think, Mommy; do you like it?"

Mrs. Kaplan sighed. "I'm reserving judgment until: a) I've seen the place, and b) I've digested both this lunch and the whole idea. It's just too totally unexpected and unbelievable. But whatever the case, the first thing we'll all do now — and I'm willing to leave the dirty dishes in the sink, mind you — is walk up there together and view the real estate. I mean, after all, we do have to consider the block, the neighborhood, the re-sale value, and so on, if our daughter is going to speculate, right?" she smiled. "Let's *bentch,* and then off we go, agreed?" She looked around the table and everyone nodded their assent.

An hour later, Mr. Kaplan and Avigayil sat at the Brinkmans' dining-room table with the owners. At short notice, and because Mr. Kaplan had to get back to the city, they had made time to discuss an unusual and intriguing request for a private 'business' session.

After the obligatory few sentences of opening banter, Avigayil's father came straight to the point.

"I'm really here only to accompany my client, a Miss A. Kaplan, and to advise her at her own discretion. She will present her proposition to you herself." He swept his arm in Avigayil's direction, as if to give her the floor.

Avigayil, who had been all through this presentation business at lunch, and had, at least, garnered some encouragement and praise at the 'Open House' later, was now more relaxed and sure of her ground. She began with the cabin.

"Pete's Place? Yes, of course," said Mrs. Brinkman. "I know the shack. I never go all the way up there — we're so busy down around here, you know. But, yes, I know it."

Mr. Brinkman, with a puzzled frown, nodded agreement.

"Could I buy it off you?" asked Avigayil.

"I beg your pardon?" Mrs. Brinkman exclaimed. "Hope you don't mind my wondering, Avi," she added. "It's not exactly the Waldorf, after all!" She smiled around the little circle as if for confirmation of her sanity.

Avigayil took a deep breath, and then launched into her pitch.

"See, I inherited some money. I got a *yerushah,* left to me by an older sister of my Bubby Kaplan," she began. "With the check, there was a letter in which she wrote that I was free to use the money any way I wanted, and for a full six months, I couldn't think of a single idea. I gave *maaser*, and we put the rest in the bank... and there it's been gathering dust, as my father says."

"And now you saw this magnificent piece of property, and that did it!" Mr. Brinkman tipped back his chair, and laughed out loud.

"When I'm done with it," said Avigayil with a brave toss of her long dark hair, "it will be!"

"Reb Velvel," murmured Mr. Brinkman *sotto voce,* with a tinge of pity, "what's gotten into your wonderful, level-headed, solid-as-a-rock oldest child, whom we've known for years and years? What IS she talking about?"

"She's really bent on doing this, Reb Yisrael, and that's the truth. I know this whole *yerushah* bit sounds like something out of a fairy tale, but it's one hundred percent real, and it's for her to spend on anything within reason that she chooses. She's got her heart set on owning this hut, fixing it up, and plenty of dreams about how to use it once it's perfect in her eyes. Provided the floors aren't rotted through, the roof doesn't leak, and the plumbing works, we've said we'll help her get it," said Mr. Kaplan.

Mrs. Brinkman cleared her throat.

"This is really quite an amazing story, and certainly a 'first' in the annals of Piney Hollow," she smiled. "However, I'm dreadfully sorry, Avi, but it's totally out of question."

Avigayil stared. "Why not?" she whispered.

"Because we have agreed between all six of us — that is, the two of us, and the two couples who are our silent partners in this bungalow colony — that we'll never sell any of the units singly. It's signed and sealed." She patted Avigayil's shoulder and sighed. "So sorry, Avi, but you do understand...?"

"But this is not one of the regular bungalows," protested Avigayil.

"True. But the agreement includes all buildings that appear on the original blueprint of the property. Right, Sruly?" She looked at her husband, seeking some help from that quarter. "That means even the casino, the *shul*, our main building, etc.... and I'm sure Pete's Place was also marked in there."

"Definitely!" said Mr. Brinkman, thoughtfully. "We even added an amendment, that anything new we might build over the years would be subject to the same rules. Still....while we're talking about this idea, I've thought about something else. How about renting it?" He looked at his wife with eyebrows raised, in inquiry. "How does that sound to you?"

Avigayil slumped in her chair. She was sure she was going to start crying in a minute. How embarrassing! Concentrate on what they're saying, she told herself. Don't give up without a fight!

"Hmm!" mused Mrs. Brinkman. "Maybe that's a possibility."

"What do you mean?" questioned Avigayil. Renting wasn't the same as owning, and as for fixing up a *rented* place — what for? This was a real blow! Somehow she'd never admitted to herself that it might not happen. She clasped her clammy hands together and looked up at Mr. Brinkman.

"Well, you could rent it for the summer, and fix it up to suit yourself. Then, at the end of the season you get first choice on it for next year, and so on and so on. I guess with Camp Zimra nearby, and Sue Kaplan being one of their most valuable staff members, you'll probably keep coming unless *Mashiach's* here first, *b'ezras Hashem*."

Mr. Kaplan was leaning forward, absorbing every word.

"It would really be almost like your own that way. You know how your family has become attached to your bungalow, and you wouldn't change it for any other? Well, this could become YOUR own bungalow in that sense, wouldn't it?" he asked Avigayil kindly.

Mrs. Brinkman sounded relieved. "I like it," she decided.

Avigayil looked at her father. He seemed interested.

"How much would you charge her?" he asked.

"Well, you've sort of caught us by surprise with all this," said Mr. Brinkman. "We'll have to think about it and consult. Maybe the first year she could have it for free in exchange for making it over, and then, next summer, we would take it from there, Kayla?" He turned to his wife.

"First I'd like to go up there with you, Avi, and Mr. Kaplan, and open it up — if we can! — to take a good look around. There's no point in spending a penny on it if it's about to collapse, right? And, if we do find it 'do-able' we can get right to it. That is, if the other partners okay it, and I don't see why they wouldn't." She put her arm around Avigayil's shoulder and gave her a hug.

Avigayil suddenly felt her spirits lifting. True, it wasn't what she'd dreamed of, and yet perhaps it would serve the same purpose.

"Could we go up there now, before my father has to get back to New York, please?" she pleaded. "If your partners agree, I mean, I'd love to get started if it is 'do-able.'"

The Brinkmans, who were by now caught up in the scheme, were tantalized by the idea of trying to pry that rusty lock open, so they could inspect a piece of their property to which they hadn't given a thought in years.

Armed with some wicked-looking tools, Mr. Brinkman led the way as they trudged up the hill, through the field, and onto the site. If anyone noticed the procession, they made no move toward them. It was only when they neared their destination that they spotted Nesanel Lowinger, with his back to them, peering through the cracked windowpanes.

"Leave him to me!" whispered Mrs. Brinkman into Avigayil's ear.

"Hi there, Nesanel!" she called from a few yards away. The boy spun around, frozen to the spot. His face was blank, but his eyes flitted from one to the other, like a wary threatened creature caught unawares. 'I dare you!' he seemed to be saying.

"Just the boy I was looking for," Mrs. Brinkman continued, unabashed. "Please run down and tell your mother that Mr. Brinkman will be there to look at your leaking faucet in a few minutes. Ask her to stay in the bungalow. We'll need her to show us what the trouble is, okay? Thanks!"

Nesanel, far from running, began to amble down the slope. There was no way of defying Mrs. Brinkman, but his departure was clearly meant to convey rebellion and bravado. He began to whistle, and turned his head several times over his shoulder to watch them.

"He's threatening us," said Mrs. Brinkman. "I've never seen so much pent-up anger in a kid that age! Okay; now, let's see."

The padlock, urged along by a few feisty squirts of lubricating oil, came loose quite easily, and the door creaked open on rusty hinges. A heady, clammy smell assailed them as they made way for Avigayil to be the first to cross the threshold.

"Something's already living here," remarked Mr. Kaplan, holding his nose. "Either dead or alive!"

The dim light from the two dusty windows revealed a good-sized area, the floor of torn linoleum piled high with discards, assorted junk and broken pieces of furniture. Against one wall, a bed-frame, strewn with mounds of ancient bedding, bore witness to Pete's very real presence here long ago. From that jumble of quilts and rags emanated an unspeakable odor. Whatever had crept in from outside had most certainly made its cozy nest right there.

Avigayil reached for the light switch beside the door, but there was no bulb in the socket of the cord dangling from a hole in the middle of the ceiling. Along the far wall ran a long wooden counter which held broken dishes and pots, and above that an electric outlet, doubtless once used for some kind of cooker. There was also a space where, long ago, the upside-down sink, now in the middle of the floor, must have been at home.

Avigayil, unperturbed by all of this, picked her way delicately, stepping around and over the debris, until she reached the door in the left corner of the room. This led into what she had supposed all along to be a bathroom. The rusty fixtures of toilet and sink were stuffed with wadded paper towelling and steel wool pads. Draped across the piled-up sink, arranged most artistically, were a pair of filthy extra-long brown shoelaces.

Shoelaces in the bathroom sink? Perhaps Pete had wanted to give them a good scrub before heading out to his new life away from here. They seemed almost like a farewell message, a signature. This, oddly enough, more than all the chaos and decay in the rest of the hut, kindled her desire anew to get her hands on this mess. She wished she could to start work that very second! Her eyes traveled up to the window high up in the rear wall that she had spotted from outside. "I'll find a step-ladder, and even get to you," she promised with a grin. "I'll have you sparkling like a diamond!"

When she returned to the main room, Mrs. Brinkman was saying, "I'd like to turn on the bathroom faucet and see if there's any water — but it's best to wait until the sink is cleaned because we might end up with a flood."

"Let's just get a trickle then, to make sure," said her husband, and he gave the handle a slight twist. Everyone stared at the ancient rusty faucet mesmerized, and, incredibly, as if their willing it had coaxed it into life, a sputter came first, then a gurgle, followed by a hiss, and then, amazingly, a thin stream of brownish water — enough to prove that the system was intact.

"Hooray!" shouted Mr. Kaplan. "It must be a good *siman*. Now we'll get a bulb and test the electricity."

Avigayil was off! She sprinted down the slope and filched a light bulb from her mother's supplies. On her way back up, she saw Nesanel not twenty feet from the cabin, sitting in the grass and keeping an eye on the goings-on.

"Hey! Didn't she say he's coming down to fix our leak?" he yelled at Avigayil. "What's happening up there, anyway?" He flung his arm out in the direction of Pete's Place.

Avigayil, huffing and puffing up the incline, refused to miss a beat; gasping for breath, she called over her shoulder, "He'll be there in five minutes," and resolutely put him out of her mind.

In no time at all, the bulb was in place, and illuminated the entire sorry scene.

"'*Vayehi Ohr!*' Beautiful!" declared Mr. Kaplan with great dramatic emphasis. "It seems that the water and electricity here are in perfect sync with the rest of the bungalows. Everything seems plausible now."

Without any of them having noticed, Mrs. Kaplan, Bubby and Shuli had followed Avigayil, and were now grouped at the entrance, totally speechless.

Shuli swallowed hard and finally asked, "What seems plausible?"

"The Avigayil Kaplan Transformation Project," intoned Bubby, bravely. "What do you say, Sue?"

Mrs. Kaplan sighed deeply. "Who'll shlep, is what I want to know. How will she get rid of all this junk?"

Mr. Brinkman scratched his head with his *yarmulke.*

"I've been thinking about that during our investigation here," he said. "You all know Tzali, my nephew and right-hand man. He's pretty busy around the place, but when he isn't working for me, you could pay him by the hour, and he'd be more than happy to make an extra few dollars in his free time. He has the use of the truck, and he'll haul the stuff away and pick up anything you order from the stores in town. Isn't that what *yerushos* are all about? I thought that's what everyone does with their loot when they inherit a fortune, right, Reb Velvel?" He slapped Mr. Kaplan on the back.

"Well, not exactly everyone, I'll admit," returned Mr. Kaplan. "Our Avigayil has always been 'interesting,' if you know what I mean. She goes her own way. Now, maybe you can get in touch with your *chevrah*, Reb Yisrael, and let us know your decision. Tzali's availability certainly puts it all into the realm of possibility." He gave one last look around, and added, "You'd better lock up by yourself, Avi, and see if you can manage this rusty contraption. But leave the key with the Brinkmans until we know for sure, okay?"

When the two families parted ways a few minutes later, Nesanel was still watching, lying on his stomach in the grass, almost hidden from view, and still as a stone.

# Chapter Ten

In the end, Shuli turned out to be the most supportive friend a sister could ever want. Truth to tell, Shuli was just a bit bored with Piney Hollow, the day-camp job, and life in general. Perhaps this 'insane' plan of Avigayil's had suddenly ignited her innate sense of adventure and fun. It certainly was different, and offered vistas of interaction with people and events heretofore unknown to any of them.

The Brinkmans had informed Avigayil that they had been able to contact one of the couples whose consent was needed. They had been amazed by this new development, but had given their whole-hearted approval and best wishes for success. The other couple, alas, was presently visiting their children in Israel, and were now on a three-day tour and could not be reached. The hotel management had promised to transmit a message for them to call the bungalow colony upon their return.

At night, Shuli offered a shoulder to cry on.

"First of all, remember they're seven hours ahead of us in *Eretz Yisrael*, right?" she reasoned. "So they're already well into their trip. Secondly, hey! You can use the waiting time to make lists. You can get organized! Know what I mean? This way, the minute you get the okay, you'll be all set to start."

"What do you mean, 'get the okay'?" moaned Avigayil, scrunching up her blanket. "They'll say no, you'll see!"

"No way!" countered Shuli, with all the assurance of a prophet. "They have nothing to lose, and lots to gain. Why should they care what happens to old Pete's palace?"

"Some guys don't like people to mess with their property, either way. They just want everything to remain '*status quo.*'" Avigayil realized even as she was arguing that she was really trying to prepare herself for the worst.

Shuli made one more stab at shoring up the crumbling fort that was her usually stalwart sister.

"Listen, whatever you do to that wreck of a place can only be an improvement. Believe me, Avi, one day they'll thank you for having noticed it in the first place. Oh, and by the way, Esti's been neglected on account of all this. She came over when you and Ta were at the main house, and told Mommy that she'd brought the stones. She was clutching a sandwich bag full of small pebbles. Whatever was that all about?" Shuli yawned with great gusto.

"Oh, wow! You're right! I've got to get to her tomorrow morning before the orders come in. Anyhow, I'll say this much. I'm going to have to work at being patient, something I'm not really cut out for." Avigayil sighed, and turned towards the wall.

"If I can get through the next few days without driving everyone crazy, I guess we can chalk one up in favor of this project before I even get started. Don't tell anyone about it, though; they'll all know soon enough if it ever gets off the ground." She sat up in bed and peered through the window. "It's pouring out there," she said wistfully. "I love the sound of heavy rain, especially in the country and most especially at night. And Shuli, thanks loads! You know, you've been a great help. Let's call it quits now; I'm going to say *Kerias Shema*."

There was no answer from the bunk bed. Shuli was fast asleep.

The week dragged on for Avigayil. Everything seemed to be moving in slow motion. Whatever she saw, whatever she heard, whatever transpired, it all seemed as though the earth's spin around the sun was reduced to half its usual speed. Did hours really tick along as if they slogged through heavy mud and couldn't make headway?

The others didn't appear to notice. Mrs. Kaplan came back and reported on her first meeting at Camp Zimra. Yes, they were indeed putting on 'Shefford' for their major performance. Someone had miraculously provided authentic snapshots taken at the time, and these were very helpful. There were some excellent pictures of the famous headmistress, Dr. Judith Grunfeld, and Mrs. Kaplan wouldn't rest until she got those clothes exactly right.

Esti persisted in hanging around and finally Avigayil realized what she must do. She went over to Mrs. Neufeld and volunteered to continue working with Esti on a steady basis each morning at ten o'clock, except for any necessary changes related to her job.

"I really appreciate this, I cannot tell you how much," said Mrs. Neufeld. "But how can I impose on anyone like that? I'd insist on paying, of course...."

"Oh, absolutely not! It'd be *you* doing *me* a favor" Avigayil insisted. "See, it's practice for me in real life, for something I might want to do when I get older. I'm asking you to give me that chance, if you really felt I could do the job. Know what I mean?"

What a speech! It was surely the longest string of words she'd ever laid before a mere acquaintance.

"Well, if you put it that way..." Mrs. Neufeld was quite flustered and at a complete loss.

Avigayil waited quietly, staring at her scuffed sneakers and biting her lip.

"I'll tell you what: Let me discuss it with Mr. Neufeld this evening, Avi, and see what he has to say." Mrs. Neufeld had gotten her second wind. "If you took it on, we'd test her once in a while, just to see how she's coming along. But whatever we decide, Avi, I want to tell you that I think you're one special, wonderful girl, and if you ever do go into teaching of some kind, your students will be the ones who lucked out!"

Next morning, Mrs. Neufeld appeared at the Kaplans' bungalow with Moishie strapped in his stroller, and Esti skipping ahead to show the way to the house where Avi lived. The deal was struck, and the little stones were set to work immediately, as tools for math in adding and subtracting. Esti thought it was the greatest fun.

"*I've* been telling *you* what to do all this time," said Avi, snatching the pebbles over to her side of the table. "Now, it's your turn!"

"One plus two?" suggested Esti doubtfully.

"Okay," said Avigayil, head bent in total concentration on the stones. She laid one stone aside, and placed a group of three others a small distance away. Then she counted slowly and clearly, pointing at each one: "one, two, three, four," and watched Esti, who was frowning.

"Wrong! Wrong! Wrong!" squealed Esti, her face turning pink. "You did one plus *three*. Do it again!"

Avi looked crestfallen; she'd made a 'boo-boo.' Quickly she did as she was told — one plus two. She pointed, counted and looked up at her coach for approval. Esti nodded vigorously, and beamed from ear to ear. It had worked!

The Brinkmans' friends returned to their hotel Wednesday morning. The next day, Avigayil finally got their approval. The man had said he'd never heard of a more fantastic story: A girl of fourteen inheriting a *yerushah*, and then this refreshingly original plan.

"Please make sure to give her a picnic table outside, like all the other bungalows have," his wife had insisted. "And I'll spend some time before we come back to get her the most divinely beautiful, most rustic *mezuzah* case that *Yerushalayim* has to offer. This kid's made my day!" she'd said, and hung up with a chuckle. Mrs. Brinkman related all this in minute detail to an ecstatic audience of one, Avigayil Kaplan.

After that precious news bulletin, time rushed in on Avigayil with the speed and power of a rough high tide. Gone was the sluggish feeling of the last few days. It was as if in one tremendous swoop, a load had been lifted from her shoulders and whisked out of sight, setting her free to sprint and win.

# *Chapter Eleven*

She used yellow rubber gloves for the wet work, and heavy gardening gloves for disposing of all the dry, smelly, rotted refuse that littered the cabin. For some reason, unclear even to herself, she had decided to hang on to Pete's brown shoelaces, which she kept soaking in a strong solution of disinfectant, stirring the brew every once in a while with a twig, a smile on her lips. All the rest of the junk was gotten rid of in a whirlwind of boundless energy.

Tzali, Mrs. Brinkman's nephew and jack-of-all-trades around the place, supplied her with huge garbage containers and recycling bins. Whenever these threatened to collapse under their odorous mounds of waste, he cheerfully carted them off in his pick-up truck and brought replacements.

"Relax!" he told her with the brightest of smiles, flashing a perfect set of teeth, a white gash between his bushy, reddish-blond beard and moustache. "Rome wasn't built in a day. Sit in the sun a bit — what's your rush? 'More haste, less speed,' get it?" He was given to sprinkling his conversations liberally with such 'meaningful sayings.' He'd amble about, all 200 roly-poly pounds of him, and heave those overflowing bins into the flat back of his truck without ever spilling a single item.

"Thanks loads, Tzali," Avigayil would answer over her shoulder, unwilling to stop her foraging to engage in aimless chatter.

"Will Rutti take me to town this afternoon, do you think?"

"Probably. She's got to go to Staples for the day camp, I know. They're forever running out of things, and they always want the stuff yesterday!" He laughed. "Tomorrow I'll try to have your new picnic table up here. Where do you want it?"

"To the left of the house. Right here!" Avigayil even took time out to point at the spot.

"No problem! It's the perfect place!" Tzali agreed. "Hey, Esti," he shouted at the little girl squatting on her haunches, studying the scurrying ants from under a stone she had just dislodged. He got down to her level and said: "Well, now, look at them hurrying and zooming around just like your friend Avigayil here. No peace — no rest — no relaxing! Very unhealthy! Here, have a lollipop." He dug into his work pants pocket and produced a dusty, bent albeit still wrapped in cellophane — lollipop. "Green okay?" he asked.

Esti nodded with great enthusiasm. "Thank you," she told him, and grabbed the bait. "The hole inside needs a sink," she added, staring at the ant colony. "I know," said Tzali, never missing a beat. "It's a scary, dark hole, but — first things first, right? When Avigayil's got it all nice and cleaned up, we'll get that sink shoved in the hole, quick as a wink. Promise!"

He rose, waved and was off.

Tzali's wife was the 'driver' for Piney Hollow. Her baby son of four months was strapped into his car seat for the greater part of each afternoon, while Rutti, who looked as if she were Tzali's twin rather than his wife, ran her errands. She was a large woman, fair and with a glorious dimpled smile for everyone. But there the similarity to her husband ended. Nimble, quick and light on her feet, she was never still for a moment. The idea of Rutti lying on a beach chair at the pool was too ludicrous to contemplate. Instead, she swam fifteen laps each morning at six, rain or shine, without fail, while Tzali and the baby were still fast asleep.

Avigayil truly enjoyed her outings with Rutti, because here was someone who understood her urgency. To her own surprise, she found herself talking quite easily with this young woman.

"I have it almost all cleaned out now," she told her older friend a week after she'd gotten her go-ahead. "My mother and I worked on a list of what to get for basics, like..."

Wails from the baby signified a dire need.

"Pacifier trouble," diagnosed Rutti. "He keeps losing his plug."

Avigayil bent over and took care of the baby, whose chin was slippery from drooling. "It just sort of slides out," she said. "He hasn't got teeth yet to chomp down on it."

"So, what's on your list?" asked Rutti.

"Well, there's the sink for the main room. Then I want to find a carpenter to run a wide ledge like a continuous counter all around the walls. For stuff, you know? And then I'll get something to sit on. I'm not quite sure yet what."

"Great! I'll drop you off at the Housewares Depot, and pick you up in an hour and a half, how's that? It'll do to get you started, I expect. Oh, did you measure for the sink?"

"Sure. You know who's good at all that?" Avigayil stole a sidelong glance at the driver. Should she share this amazing piece of information with an outsider? Rutti's gaze never wavered from the road.

"Who?" she asked.

"Nesanel Lowinger," Avigayil told her. "He's been hanging around and watching. That's also something he's fabulous at! Half the time he's watching from a hiding place. But that's beside the point. He's really quite brilliant, I think. Very good at all kinds of odd jobs, especially anything that needs a brain — like, for example, measuring." She shook her head in wonder, and then continued, "Please, Rutti, not a word about this to anyone. He'd be furious if people knew he could be normal and even helpful when he wants to be. It means everything to him to preserve his horrible reputation."

Rutti placed her finger on her lips. "I never heard!" she said. "But…just between the two of us, I'm shocked. I thought there's nothing about that kid that could possibly work. Being proved wrong is a real lesson for me. '*al tistakel bakankan, ela bemah sheyesh bo*,' right? You're not supposed to judge a person by what you see on the outside! Good luck, Avi; between Esti Neufeld and Nesanel, you've got your work cut out for you. Okay, I'll let you off here. See you later! Have fun!" And with a firm step on the accelerator, she was gone.

Mr. Kaplan, afraid that the various stores might not be willing to accept his credit card from the hands of his fourteen-year-old daughter, had left a sufficient sum of cash for Avigayil to use. She entered the huge store on the outskirts of town, feeling both elated and very apprehensive at the same time. 'Everyone must be staring at me,' she thought. 'They must all be wondering, "What on earth is this kid doing in a place like this?"'

She had managed to scrub out and bleach the bathroom sink and toilet, which now gleamed white and shiny, almost like new. She had decided to buy a set of faucets for the little sink, and a new toilet seat. Also, of course, there was the big sink to get, complete with fixtures and an enclosed cabinet beneath. These items would be more than enough to keep her busy for the allotted time.

The middle-aged sales lady who came to her assistance was in her element. How energizing, in the middle of another boring, routine day, to find a young teenager shopping for items that were usually never purchased by anyone under thirty. The woman had haggled with retired couples who were redoing their homes, and who thought the 'new' prices outrageous. She saw plumbers, their work clothes shiny with grease, popping chewing gum with every half-sentence, or weary, distracted young mothers, trying to focus on the pros and cons of stainless steel versus enamel, while their little angels scampered off in all directions and needed lassoing back. This, on the other hand, was a refreshing experience, and she gave Avigayil all her attention and the benefit of her years of expertise.

Having left a fifty-dollar deposit with the address of Piney Hollow Bungalow Colony, Avigayil then tucked the receipt into her waist pack and stepped outside into the sunshine, flushed and bursting with the exciting prospect of telling Mommy and Shuli all about everything at supper tonight.

After having taken care of the bigger items, the sales clerk had steered her to a special section of reduced fixtures. She had been able to find a very pretty set of faucets with wood handles at half-price for the bathroom, and a nice deal on the high, swiveling one-arm contraption for the bigger sink. Next time there, she would do some exploring on lighting fixtures or reading lamps.

Rutti drove up almost immediately. This time, Dovi was fast asleep.

"My mother won't let me stay up there over night," Avigayil told Rutti in a whisper, so as not to disturb the little boy. She buckled herself in and settled back. "I suppose she's right. It's too far up the back field for anyone to hear me if I yelled for help," she sighed.

"*Chas v'shalom!*" Rutti sounded appalled. "Of course she's right — and it's adjacent to the woods, too! Will Tzali pick up your stuff tomorrow?"

"I hope so," replied Avigayil. "It always depends on the Brinkmans, you know? They get him first," she added wistfully. "Without the two of you, I could have never even attempted the project. I'm so grateful!"

"No problem," said Rutti, as she turned on the windshield wipers. "Not only Nesanel, but the entire Piney Hollow, is watching you with bated breath. It's the first interesting thing going on around here for years. We were in a serious rut until now. Hey! Take a look at that sky! Ten minutes ago it was blue, without a cloud to be seen, and now — whoa! I'm glad we're not far from home."

# *Chapter Twelve*

**E**sti loved the new picnic-table. Even though it was identical to theirs 'at home,' this one was brand-new, and above all, empty!

"At our house," she told Avigayil, "I hafta sit at the end of the bench, and they keep shoving and pushing me off."

"With all of you having to eat at the same time, I can see where that might be a problem," said Avigayil. "It's not really their fault, it's just crowded."

"But here I can sit on any side I want, and at the ends and in the middle, and it smells all new." She bent low over the table and gave a deep, delighted sniff. "Yum!" she exclaimed.

She was speaking in longer sentences now, and with far greater confidence. Her work was progressing at a remarkable rate, with Avigayil covering a lot more ground than the daily assignments required. She forged ahead, dreaming up new ways to increase Esti's proficiency in all areas, while the little girl thought they were just playing and having a wonderful time.

"You won't believe it," said Avigayil, home for a short lunch break, to her mother. "But sometimes I'd give anything just to cut Esti's time short, or cancel altogether. I'm so busy with the cabin, it's a real challenge not to let everything else go down the drain. But I've taken her on, and I do get to *shep* a lot of *nachas,* too."

She looked at her mother, who was sketching designs for the clothing to be worn by the non-Jewish housewives, who took the little Jewish children into their homes in Shefford during the war. Was she listening to her? The performance was scheduled for two weeks from now, and time was running out. Her mother probably hadn't heard a word she'd said.

"I bet that's exactly how the people in the small villages in England felt about having all these Jewish kids from London dumped on their doorsteps. 'What on earth are they doing to us here?' they wondered. 'What are those things with strings these boys wear under their shirts, and why can't they switch off their own bedroom lights on a Friday night? Let's just cancel, and give them the heave-ho. We've got enough on our plates; goodness gracious, there's a war on!' "

Mrs. Kaplan did a perfect job of mimicking Bubby's still-intact English accent. "But there you are. They'd been recruited and had said 'yes,' and they stuck with it! As the story goes in the end they, too, derived *nachas* in their own way." Mrs. Kaplan smiled.

Avigayil wasn't giving up so fast. "Maybe at least the Brinkmans could find someone else to do the orders? I mean, it's all set up and running smoothly by now, more or less," she sighed.

Mrs. Kaplan, tapping her pencil against her teeth, held her sketchbook up and studied it critically. "Listen," she said, "once you've got your place in good shape, you'll be able to fit all that in without a problem. It's a few weeks — maybe two or three? — of pressure from all sides right now. Believe me, I know all about pressure." And that was that, thought Avigayil, and as usual, her mother had a point.

Already the plumbing was in place. A carpenter had installed an eighteen-inch ledge of a light pumpkin-colored formica along both long sides of the room. Today the linoleum was going to be put down. Avigayil couldn't wait! Automatically fingering the large key to the old rusty lock, which she now always wore on a string around her neck, she started up the slope through the field.

When she got three-quarters of the way to the hut, she thought she saw Nesanel bent over the picnic table, working at something. But by the time she reached the top, he was sitting there staring blankly into space.

"Got a job?" he asked, avoiding direct eye contact, as if to protect himself from appearing too eager.

He really wasn't a bad-looking boy at all, Avigayil decided. His hair was thick and dark. Behind his glasses, his hazel eyes surveyed the world with great intelligence, and often cunning. Those eyes could turn ice-cold or into slits of rage when he felt threatened. But Avigayil had sometimes seen them wide open, innocent, and even trusting.

She often thought that one of the reasons he was such a misfit with his peers was that his mother insisted on dressing him as she did. Today he wore a light blue long-sleeved shirt, starched and ironed; dark charcoal corduroy pants; and shiny black lace-up shoes. Later she would wonder what had prompted her to study his clothes so intently on that particular day. 'Poor kid,' thought Avigayil, eyeing her own dirty sneakers, black denim skirt, and well-worn plaid shirt. 'It's a wonder he puts up with such nonsense.'

"The floor guys will be here any moment. They may have to tear out the old linoleum, in which case I have a wonderful job for you. We'll both have to say *Tehillim* that I won't have to have a sub-floor put in before they lay down the new one. That would cost a mint!" She laughed. "Don't worry, I'm just kidding!"

"What's a sub-floor?"

"You'll see soon enough if you stick around, and if I'm out of luck," said Avi as she unlocked the door and vanished inside.

The place looked cool, bare and light. After the men left, maybe early tomorrow, she'd start painting the walls. The cans of paint — pale yellow brushes, roller and tray, sat ready on the work counter near the new sink. She had already pried off the lids and used the wooden spatula they had given her to stir the paint thoroughly. Carefully folding some clean squares of gauze over the two gallon containers, she replaced the lids lightly on top, to keep everything in place. Tzali had promised to do the ceilings, but she was determined to do the rest. Rags, drop cloths and plastic tablecloths to be draped over the counters were all neatly stacked in the cabinet under the sink.

When she heard the van pull up, she stepped outside and looked around for Nesanel. He was nowhere to be seen; probably lurking somewhere — it was his favorite pastime!

There were two men who seemed friendly enough, but in a bit of a rush.

"All ready for us?" the tall, skinny one wanted to know.

Avigayil nodded, and gestured for them to go inside and look around.

After a cursory glance, they got down on their hands and knees, prodded and pulled, peered into corners, and examined the little bathroom.

"It'll do," said Skinny. "We can lay it right over the old one. What d'ya say, Jake?"

"It'll never get more traffic than two months out of the year, and not much even then. It's tiny! Sure, let's go!"

They unloaded her beautiful linoleum, dark green with flecks of lighter green, soft yellow, orange and white, and with a deep, rich luster. This would definitely be the one biggest expense of the whole project, and it had to be perfect! Avigayil mustered all her courage to make certain it would be.

"Are you sure if you leave this old brown thing underneath, there won't be bumps and stuff afterwards? See, I'm paying for this out of my own pocket, and I really care how it's going to look and wear. Know what I mean?"

Skinny regarded his partner.

"She's paying, Jake. Let's give her our super-deluxe job, okay? Not to worry, young lady," he smiled, turning to Avigayil. "If we made a mess of this, you'd be back in the store to complain, quick as a wink, and we'd be out of a job, right? Our boss expects us to deliver the goods, and we've both been with him — yikes, I don't even want to think back how many years it's been. Hey, how come YOU'RE paying for this?"

"It's a long story," Avigayil told him with a grin, "and I know you're in a hurry, so I don't want to hold you up. How long will it take, do you think?"

"Oh, about two hours or so," replied Skinny, who seemed to be the one to make decisions. "You come and check up on us every once in a while." He pulled out his bill of delivery, and peered at the addressee. "Ms. Avigayil Kaplan?"

"You bet!" said Avigayil, and with a wave and smile, she started down towards home.

That evening Avigayil held 'Open House' for her mother and Shuli.

"Avi, it's stupendous!" exclaimed Mrs. Kaplan.

"Amazing!" gasped Shuli.

"I'll help you paint, if you can bear to have me around, that is," she added, as they stood under the single dangling light bulb that still served as the only illumination in the cabin. "It's totally stunning! How did you pick this floor? I mean how did you go about deciding which to choose? I *love* it!"

"Me, too," said Mommy. "The whole place is already beautiful."

"To tell you the truth, it chose me. Does that sound crazy? But it really did! Out of all the millions of patterns, this one sort of sang out to me: 'I'm the one that looks like your field, green and full of flowers. Or maybe I'm like a sunny patch in Piney Woods. Pick me, and I'll bring the outdoors right into your living room!' And I knew that's exactly what I wanted."

Avigayil looked at them to gauge their reactions. She had uncharacteristically been able to share something from deep inside her with them. It felt good. She giggled, knowing she wasn't brave enough yet to tell them about her whimsical plan to have Tzali paint the ceilings sky blue!

"I'll get started on the walls early tomorrow. Tuesday there are no orders, just Esti. Thanks tons, Shuli. When you're through with camp come and paint; by that time I'll be zonked," said Avigayil.

෬ඊ෮෮ ෬ඊ෮෮ ෬ඊ෮෮

She got up at six in the morning, *davened* and left the house twenty minutes later. The mist lifting from the meadow was like a sheer veil, lit from behind by the palest of early morning sunlight. With every step she took, the grass beneath her, still drenched in dew, bent and flattened underfoot. From the woods came the dawn chorus of birds greeting the new day. The radio had predicted a sweltering ninety-eight degrees, even in the mountains. It would be a scorcher! For a moment she took time to turn around, and survey 'her' domain from up here. The colony was still sound asleep. She made out the solitary figure of Rutti on her way to the pool, carrying a bright red towel around her shoulders. The men, studying the *Daf Yomi*, were probably already learning in the *shul*. In another hour or so the place would become a beehive of activity.

As soon as she came level with the hut, she felt a stab of panic. Why was the door wide open? She broke into a run, her heart pounding. At the top she braked, and stared into the room, her hand clapped over her mouth, in horror.

"Oh, no!" she wailed out loud. "Oh, no! No! No!" Yellow paint was spilled all across her brand-new floor. She stepped gingerly inside. More paint spattered the shiny sink. The work counter was smeared and streaked, paint dripping, with thin rivulets leading all the way into the bathroom. The paint containers lay on the floor, empty; with tray, roller, brushes, spatula, and wadded gauze scattered here, there, and everywhere, in the rapidly congealing gooey mess. 'Let it be a bad dream,' thought Avigayil, 'a nightmare.' But the smell of fresh paint was everywhere — it was real, all right.

She clutched her arms tightly around her to give herself the comfort of their hold. Her heart actually hurt. 'So this is what they mean by heartache,' she thought, as tears began to spill over and run down her cheeks. In bitter anguish she stood and let her eyes roam over the devastation, and when she finally turned back towards the door she realized that the lock hung open on its hinge.

"It's my own fault!" She choked the words out, between racking sobs. "I left the door open."

Once again, she stepped carefully into the room, avoiding the puddles of paint as best as she could, and managed to fish a clean rag out of the box from under the sink. She let the cold water run in the bathroom, and washed her face, over and over, until she felt herself becoming calmer.

Finally she went outside, settled herself at the picnic table, and slowly began to reason and plan. 'I'll go step by step and see what happens,' she decided.

Obviously when they had left last night, she had forgotten to lock up. Nor had her mother or Shuli reminded her, but never mind about that. It wasn't a part of their routine as it was of hers.

Somebody had taken advantage of this oversight and done this horrendous thing.

This somebody had to have been aware that the door had been left open. That was surprising! After all, it had been dark by then.

The paint, still wet, was rapidly drying and crusting. So this crime, for that was how she saw it, had been perpetrated only a few hours ago.

Who might have been hiding and watching, unseen by the three of them?

Who indeed?

Was there anyone who hated her enough to cause her so much pain?

Had she been wrong all along in seeing some good in Nesanel or in thinking that she was ever so slowly cracking his armor? Had she been indulging in wishful thinking, or perhaps it had been her inflated ego claiming that she could achieve with him what no one else could? "Got a job?" he'd asked, and then, with genuine interest (or so she'd been naïve enough to believe), "What's a subfloor?"

She watched a couple of blue jays pecking in the dirt, cawing and chattering, without a care in the world. Lucky them! She took a deep breath; what was she to do? She mustn't get sidetracked. 'Concentrate!' she told herself firmly.

The paint she had picked was latex-based and therefore

washable. This at least she knew was certain, because she had specifically asked about how to clean the equipment, and they'd told her to use plain warm water and soap.

With great effort and hard work, the place could probably be cleaned up pretty well. But it had to be done now. If the paint had time to dry and set, it would be almost impossible to remove without a trace.

With that thought she jumped to her feet and began to jog to the line of bungalows, and then straight down the path to the main house. Panting and perspiring, she landed at Mrs. Brinkman's office door. It was too early, not even seven o'clock; they must still be at breakfast.

Avigayil tiptoed up to the kitchen and knocked timidly, still breathing heavily from the long run.

"Come in, " she heard Mrs. Brinkman call out. She mumbled a silent prayer and went inside.

The minute Mrs. Brinkman set eyes on the girl, she dropped her stirring spoon on the counter, wiped her hands on the kitchen towel and snapped, "Sit down!" Staring at Avigayil, she pulled a chair up for herself. "What on earth?" she whispered.

It didn't take all that long. Hiccuping now and then and trying to be coherent, Avigayil told her story.

"I need help. I don't think I can handle this on my own," she finished. She realized she sounded pretty hysterical, but she was past caring.

"The paint is drying up fast, and it'll be a big job. Do you have any cleaning help I could sort of borrow?" she gulped. "Of course I'll pay. It's all my own fault anyway; I left the door unlocked last night," she shuddered.

"Oh, Avi! I'm so sorry!" cried Mrs. Brinkman. "But first you must have a drink of water." She hurried to fill a tall glass with ice water from the refrigerator and waited for Avigayil to take a long drink.

"Now give me a second to rearrange things here," she said, pulling over the Days' Plan Book for the workers of Piney Hollow. "Okay, let me see. I'll send Eva and Manuel up there right away. They were scheduled to do the *shul* this morning, but we'll get to that later." She grabbed the mike, and called for the couple to come to the main house at once.

Avigayil began crying quietly, sniffing and blowing her nose. She was furious at herself for being so weak, but she couldn't stop.

"I don't know how to thank you," she managed to get out between sobs. "I'm so mad at myself!"

"Now stop that!" scolded Mrs. Brinkman gently. "I'm happy to have these guys available. They're very thorough and not lazy. They hate cleaning the shul, I know that, and this will make a nice change for them. A challenge, shall we say?" She laughed. "Hey, Avi! Stop bashing yourself. None of us are perfect; we all mess up once in a while. Look at the bright side — it could've been oil-based paint! Ugh!"

Avigayil grinned through her tears.

"Do you have any idea who could have done this, Mrs. Brinkman? Was there anyone you know of who was against my fixing up Pete's place?"

Before Mrs. Brinkman could answer, the Spanish-speaking couple appeared at the door, and received their orders in a mixture of English, Spanish, and a great deal of pointing and gesturing.

"Go up there with them, Avi, and show them the whole sorry story. Then they'll come back down and get the supplies they'll need. Wanna wash your face?" She rummaged in a drawer. "Here's a clean towel. Go ahead and use our bathroom, second door on your left down the hall."

Leading the way up the slope, Avigayil saw that indeed, by now, the colony had come to life. In fact, there seemed to be more activity than was usual for that time of day. She decided not to stop at home to break the bad news. There was time for that later, she thought.

First things first!

# Chapter Thirteen

As soon as Mrs. Brinkman had turned her back on the strange threesome, the door burst open again. This time it was her husband, totally distraught.

"Nesanel Lowinger's gone," he said, his face ashen, the skin stretched tightly across his cheekbones.

"What do you mean, 'gone'?" asked Mrs. Brinkman.

"Gone, as in G-O-N-E," stated Mr. Brinkman. "We've been searching for half an hour already. Mrs. Lowinger came down to the *shul* to see if he was there, and told us he hadn't been in his bed when she went in to wake him."

"Don't worry about *that* character," muttered his wife, waving her hand in dismissal. "He's around some place; he'll turn up like a bad penny."

"It's not that simple." Mr. Brinkman dabbed at his damp forehead with a handkerchief that had seen better days. "We'll have to organize a search, and make sure to cover every inch of this colony. I'm going to enlist anyone on two legs to help us find him. We'll divide up the property and have small groups for each section. In a few minutes I expect they'll all be here."

He slumped down on a chair. "Mind making me a coffee, strong and black, Kayla? This is really getting to me. That boy's been nothing but a headache from the day he set foot here," he added under his breath.

Twenty minutes later, Avigayil's mother, Mrs. Breich, and Mrs. Handelsman were dispatched to search the back field, from right to left and all the way to the outermost boundary of Piney Hollow.

The first inkling that anything was amiss reached Avigayil when she heard her mother call Nesanel's name. She was helping the young couple by spreading dripping wet cloths over the drying paint, to keep it moist enough to be removed without such scrubbing as would damage the floor permanently.

She lifted her head and listened. Yes! There it was again, and coming closer. Avigayil stepped outside to investigate. She almost collided with her mother, who, in turn, was staring in disbelief at the chaos in the cabin.

"Oh, my goodness! What's going on here? Am I dreaming or did this really happen?" she gasped.

More cries for Nesanel could be heard from across the fields, carried clearly on the motionless air of the sweltering morning.

"I'll explain in a minute," said Avigayil, "but first tell me why the whole world needs Nesanel today."

"He's vanished," sighed her mother. "No trace of him anywhere. We've been searching high and low ever since breakfast.

Everyone's pulling together. Shuli and Chevy Gordon are running the day camp all by themselves today, to free others up and to keep the kids busy so they don't get in the way. No luck yet! Okay, now please tell me what all this is about." She laid her arm across her daughter's shoulders.

Avigayil told her story for the second time that morning but, miraculously, there was a difference. She had regained her sense of being on top of things. It was already clear that long, hard work would do wonders. Manuel and Eva understood there was no time for breaks. It could only be done by relentlessly keeping at it before the paint hardened.

The heat was unbearable, and all four people present were dripping with perspiration, but all were unwilling to stop their tasks even for as long as it would take to wash up or take a drink.

"Mommy, look very carefully behind any rocks and bushes, but especially around this cabin. That boy loves to hide out nearby.

"Actually, if he had anything to do with this paint job, he's not going to be in the immediate vicinity right now ..." said Mrs. Kaplan, wiping her forehead on her sleeve. "Avi, you don't think he....?"

"Ma, when the place is cleaned up, and notice I said 'when,' I'm going to zero in on that. Right now I'm just concentrating on what can be salvaged here. *Baruch Hashem*, the Brinkmans let me have these two helpers. They're the greatest! Without them — forget it!"

Before she turned back into the hut she asked, "How's his mother taking it?"

Mrs. Kaplan called back over her shoulder, "She's fantastic! You wouldn't believe it!" and she was off striding out towards the boundary.

At one o'clock everyone met again at the main house, exhausted and defeated. Even Mrs. Brinkman, the skeptic, was now convinced that they had better call the police. All of them had done their utmost, as neighbors and friends, but they were not professionals. Mr. Brinkman reluctantly agreed, and after thanking everyone profusely, he sent them on their way, explaining that perhaps it would be best for them to stay on the grounds in case the police needed any of them for questioning. The only one to remain in the haven of the air-conditioned office with the Brinkmans was Mrs. Lowinger, who expected her husband to join them from New York at any moment.

"I didn't see Tzali here," she remarked.

Mr. Brinkman sat down behind the desk and reached for the phone.

"He's out on the golf cart. That one doesn't give up so easily! Okay, here I go." He dialed, and then slowly and clearly explained the situation, while his eyes strayed to the double window, overlooking his little realm.

One other person had remained at the main house. Avigayil sat on the back steps of the porch, nursing a bottle of ice-cold Snapple. Her job at the cabin was done. Everything was spotless, and Manuel had left Eva to shine the sink and wax the floor, just for extra protection. Avigayil had taken great pains to show her exactly how she was to lock up securely when she was finished. They had worked for hours, but it had paid off. When Tatty and Bubby arrived for Shabbos, they wouldn't suspect the disaster that had occurred.

One thing, though, had been nagging at the back of her mind. When she had examined the mess around the sink, she had not found the little dish in which the long brown shoelaces had been soaking. This bothered her; perhaps it was connected in some way with the vandalism. But its disappearance was odd: who would want such junk? She wasn't even sure why she herself had kept them, except perhaps as a souvenir of the place's history. What could it mean?

When she heard the police car pull up at the front, she scurried up the steps and slipped through the back door. While Mr. and Mrs. Brinkman ushered the two officers into the building, she managed to get inside the office and leaned unobtrusively against the far wall, quietly observing.

The older of the two men was business-like to the point of brusqueness. He nodded at the Brinkmans and curtly introduced himself and his partner.

"Sergeant Conrad and Officer McDavid. Let's sit."

Mr. Brinkman gestured to the chairs.

"Thanks for coming so promptly. By the way, this is the boy's mother, Mrs. Lowinger," he said.

The Sergeant acknowledged the introduction by turning towards her. "Now, let's be precise in our answers. Time's of the essence! "Name?"

"Nesanel Lowinger," she replied in an unwavering voice.

"Spell that," and she did.

"Age?" The man never used two words if one would suffice.

"Eight and a half."

"Physical appearance?"

"He has dark hair, glasses, hazel eyes, slim build and weighs about sixty pounds." She dug into her purse on the floor beside her, and produced a wallet from which she extracted a photo of Nesanel. "This is a school picture, taken in June," she said, handing it to the sergeant.

The younger officer, who was only about twenty-five or so, had curly red hair and a kindly manner. As soon as the questioning began, he produced a little notebook and started writing. Every once in a while, he gave them all an encouraging smile.

"Mother," came the clipped speech of the sergeant, "when did you last see the boy?"

"Last night, at nine or a quarter after. He said he was tired, went into his bedroom, and closed the door. This morning I went in to wake him up for morning services, and he wasn't in his bed."

"Yes?" Conrad never took his eyes off her.

"In fact," she continued, "he hadn't slept under his covers or changed into his pajamas. Wherever he went, he must have worn the same clothes he had on yesterday. I checked and there's nothing missing except a lightweight navy windbreaker."

"Clothes description?"

"Well, I'm not entirely sure which shirt?...." This was the first time Mrs. Lowinger faltered.

Avigayil stepped away from the wall.

"Excuse me," she said. "I know what he wore."

Sergeant Conrad turned toward her, raising his eyebrows. "Who are you?"

"A friend," she replied, shrugging her shoulders.

"Go on."

"He wore a long-sleeved light blue shirt, dark charcoal-gray corduroy pants, and shiny lace-up black oxfords."

Mrs. Lowinger stared at her, mouth agape.

"Oh, yes, I almost forgot also a black velvet yar...I mean one of those skullcaps. And sorry, but I can't tell you the color of his socks." Avigayil was done.

"Jerry," Sergeant Conrad instructed the young man, "take down her name and particulars before we leave. Let's make sure we get her right after high school. I want to hire this girl — she's got what it takes. Better by far than some of those knuckle-heads on the force."

Jerry grinned.

"How do you know all this?" Conrad asked.

Avigayil was ready. "I observed him closely yesterday, and his mother says he didn't change." Now she was grinning, too. Jerry continued to write.

Facing Mrs. Lowinger, the Sergeant asked:

"Did he take anything besides the jacket? Food? Drinks?"

"Sorry, but I didn't think to check," said Mrs. Lowinger, blushing and flustered now.

"Why do you think he might have disappeared? Any ideas, Mother?"

In a subtle way he was trying to lay the blame at her door, thought Avigayil. Mrs. Lowinger shook her head.

"Mr. Brinkman?"

"None."

"Mrs. Brinkman?"

One could sense a moment's hesitation here. Mrs. Brinkman would have said a thing or two, but there was the poor lady, and no one wanted want to add to her discomfort.

"I'm stumped," she stated. And then she added thoughtfully, "He wasn't always very happy here, I'm sure. But I can't think of any one isolated incident that would make him run away right now."

Avigayil realized she was sweating in spite of the air-conditioning. A wave of nausea washed over her, and her legs felt unsteady. She gripped the back of a chair to steady herself.

"What was he doing yesterday, Mother?"

Avigayil thought she would explode. 'She's *not* your mother; don't call her that!' she fumed inside.

"As far as I know, it was much like any other day," replied Mrs. Lowinger, having regained her equilibrium in spite of all the bashing. "I think he is fascinated with Avigayil's new project. She's renovating an old shack up on the property and he likes to hang around and watch the workers. Probably that's when Avi saw him up close yesterday. What Mrs. Brinkman said is true, by the way. It's always been hard for Nesanel to make friends. But I think he likes Avi and also Tzali, the Brinkmans' nephew. He likes being with him in his workshop."

'Whew' thought Avi. The decision had been made for her.

She still felt a little woozy, but at least she wasn't going to have to let Mrs. Lowinger in on the 'one isolated incident'!"

"Jerry?"

"Shouldn't we question this 'Sally' or whatever, I mean, the nephew, sir?"

"Where is he?" asked the Sergeant.

"Still out combing the area in the golf cart," Mr. Brinkman answered. "We can have him call the station the minute he returns."

"Do that!" The Sergeant snapped out of his chair, and almost stood at attention. "I'll put some men on the job within the hour, acting on the premise that he cannot be found on your property, right?" He addressed this to Mr. Brinkman.

"Right! Appreciate that!"

Avigayil suppressed a smile. Mr. Brinkman, unconsciously she supposed, was adopting Conrad's abrupt, staccato speech.

By three o'clock, ten officers had been assigned to the case. They fanned out over a network of streets and highways, cruising in unmarked cars or walking into garages, malls and little stores, showing copies of Mrs. Lowinger's picture.

Three specially trained men, leading police dogs to sniff the boy's scent, began the long trek into Piney Woods. The large dogs had been taken into Nesanel's bedroom to pick up the scent from his bedding and clothing. Many of the younger children in the nearby bungalows had been reduced to hysterical terror and crying fits. It took all the patience and firmness of their mothers to calm them down while trying to hide their own feelings of mounting anxiety. Mr. Lowinger, who had long since arrived, insisted on joining the team with the dogs. He simply refused to be talked out of it.

It was an endless afternoon, a draining, fear-filled evening, and a dreadful night. Somehow word had gotten around, and the men on the staff of Camp Zimra and those of Siegel's

Bungalows, five miles down the road, had converged upon Piney Hollow, equipped with food, thermos bottles of coffee and soup, flashlights and extra batteries, and bottled water. They, too, joined the throng of searchers in the woods and throughout the State Park.

The police, at times irritated by all this lay activity, nevertheless had to admit that these Jewish folk had a lot of initiative, spunk and sheer good will. It was decided to mobilize this small army and direct the efforts of the men, since it became clear that they would not be turned away in any case.

People who weren't out on the trail were doing their part by reciting *Tehillim*. Zeidy Breich, who had been a principal in an elementary yeshivah all his working life, had his own ideas. He sent word to every boy between the ages of seven and twelve to meet at his bungalow, where he himself would lead their *tefillos*. Avigayil watched from the glider on her front porch as Yanky Neufeld, Zecharia Gordon, and all the others trooped to the house next door, clutching their little *sifrei Tehillim* and dragging their heels

'What's going on in their minds right now?' wondered Avigayil. 'They must be having mixed feelings. He's their sworn enemy, but which of them would truly want to see him lost or hurt, *chas v'shalom*? Are they uneasy, suspecting that perhaps it was their own attitudes, and lack of trying to bridge the gap, that caused Nesanel to quit and run?'

Esti came over quietly and snuggled down in the glider beside her.

"Where's Nesanel?" she whispered.

"Wish I knew. Probably went for a long hike," she answered, squeezing Esti's little hand. "He'll be back very soon, *b'ezras Hashem*. When you wake up tomorrow morning, I bet he'll be home. You'd better go to your mother now, 'cause my mother, Shuli and I are going over to sit with Mrs. Lowinger until he walks in. Okay?" she gently propelled the little girl in the direction of her own home, reached for a *Siddur*, and rushed over to the Lowingers, where her mother and Shuli were already settled in at the kitchen table.

"They'll find him soon now, with so many helpers," her mother was saying, stopping to put the kettle on to boil yet again. "Don't worry, Bas Sheva! Oh, here's Avi. Come and join us."

Mrs. Lowinger's light blue eyes never wavered. The sweetest smile lit up her face.

"Hello, Avi. So nice of you to look in." Even under all the stress, she was the perfect lady.

"I'm not worried, Sue. I know Hashem won't let him come to harm."

The two girls looked at her in awe and wonder.

"You know my name's Bas Sheva," Mrs. Lowinger continued. "I was the seventh of the Adler girls on Bedford Avenue in Williamsburg. When my father was *niftar*, there were still three of us unmarried. It put a great responsibility and strain on our mother to carry on alone. But she worked hard, and we managed with the help of Hashem. Finally, there were just the two of us. My sisters were all busy with their growing families, and that left Mama and me pretty much to our own devices."

Mrs. Kaplan set a steaming cup of coffee in front of her.

"Thanks, Sue. It's nice being served in one's own kitchen," she said. "When I finally married my husband, I was almost thirty years old. Mama came to live in the apartment below ours, and things were good. But while my six sisters had many children, *b'li ayin hora*, I remained childless, and the house was serene, but quiet — oh, so quiet!"

She took a sip of coffee and sighed.

"I often thought Hashem wanted me to take care of Mama, and that is why things were the way they were. But finally the miracle happened, a true *nes*, and we were granted the blessing of having Nesanel. When he was born my husband was fifty and I was forty. Mama lived for two more years, and had the pleasure of holding him in her arms. So you see," she said, looking at all three of them in turn, with wide, shining eyes, "Hashem won't allow that child to be harmed. He was a special gift, and I have full *bitachon* that we are meant to raise him to become a wonderful *eved Hashem*, of whom we, and all of *Klal Yisrael*, will be proud."

"We're with you all the way," said Mrs. Kaplan feelingly. "Bas Sheva, you're quite an inspiration, to put it mildly. We can all learn from you."

And while the search continued through the night, spreading out over an ever-widening area, the little groups, in the privacy of their bungalows, *davened*, waited, and pondered. Did he run away, or did he just wander off and get lost? Is he hiding deliberately, and if so, why? How had he left his house without waking his mother? If he hadn't slept in his bed all night, where exactly had he been? Where was he at one, two, three, four o'clock in the middle of the night?

Nobody slept except, blessedly, the very young and the very old. Mr. Brinkman sat in his office manning the phones, in constant touch with Sergeant Conrad, who had been appointed to head the S.O.S. operation from headquarters, and who, in turn, communicated with all the officers on patrol via cell phones.

At five-thirty, just before sunrise, the first sign of hope was reported. Two of the dogs seemed to have picked up the scent. They were straining at their leashes, and pulling in the direction of the State Park Lake, leaving the thick forest of pine trees behind. It seemed that at last there was a sign of hope ... only one chilling thought marred their optimism.

"Can he swim?" Conrad asked Mr. Brinkman.

"No idea," answered Mr. Brinkman. "But I'm not about to

ask his mother that question now, believe me!" Just find him on dry land, he prayed.

And as the sun sent its first rosy glow over the lake, Tzali and Mr. Lowinger spotted him. It was the bright speck of blue in the last rowboat tied up at the dock that caught Tzali's attention. There were a great number of boats made secure for the night; paddle boats, canoes and single and double rowboats. With the ongoing heat wave and absence of recent rain they were rocking gently in the shallow water. All oars and life jackets had, of course, been stowed away and locked up in the boathouse. It was typical of Nesanel that he had picked his bunk for the night with intelligence and foresight. Rowboats had by far the most ample room for him to stretch his limbs, and higher sides than the canoes to protect him from the lapping wavelets.

Running down the sandy path, they finally reached him. He was curled up on his side, the light jacket rolled up under his head for a pillow, sleeping soundly. The rise and fall of his chest moved in time to the gentle roll of the small craft. In silence they gazed upon him, mutely uttering their prayers of thanks; the father's tears spilling down his stubbly cheeks and into his neatly trimmed graying beard. He made no move to stop them. It helped to just let go.

Tzali was the first to touch the child on the shoulder, and then, tenderly, to stroke his cheek.

"Good morning, Nesanel. Time for *Shacharis*," he said.

Slowly, Nesanel opened his eyes, and then blinked himself awake. An instant later he was sitting upright, ramrod straight, holding on to the sides of the boat to steady himself, staring at his father.

"Hi, Ta," he said, a tentative smile playing at the corners of his lips.

"Hi, *Boychik*!" said his father, his voice cracking with emotion. "*Baruch Hashem, Baruch Hashem*! You're safe and we found you!"

"Hey, Nesanel, first things first," said Tzali, all business. "*Modeh Ani* and *negel vasser*!" Miraculously he produced a tin cup from his own backpack. "Just dip and help yourself. There's no shortage of water around here, as you can see." He laughed at his own display of normalcy. He handed the cup to Nesanel, who grinned and washed his hands. Then, grabbing the jacket, he jumped out of the boat, onto the pier, and faced the mass of humanity that was quickly gathering momentum.

Police and laymen were streaming to the water's edge, as cameras flashed and dogs barked. Over his loudspeaker in the car, Officer McDavid announced the end of the search, thanking one and all for their tireless help and selfless efforts. "Let's not forget our wonderful dogs, Rush and Bushy, who worked so hard and led us to this spot. And now, if you'll make way here, I'll drive this young man back home to his Mom, who, I'm sure, can't wait another minute."

Tzali sat in front with the officer, and Nesanel cuddled up to his father in the back. He was thoroughly bedraggled, and suddenly, looking down at his filthy clothes, the enormity of this entire episode engulfed him. He was weak and hungry, tired and anxious, suspicious of what he would find at the colony, and, oh yes! He felt exactly eight-and-a-half years old, and not a day older.

By the time they reached Piney Hollow, the entire colony was gathered in front of the main house, singing and dancing. Zeidy Breich, in his wheel chair, led the impromptu choir, while the Brinkmans handed out ice-cold drinks — on the house! — to one and all. Avigayil thought the relief and joy in that crowd was so real, you could almost touch it!

Mrs. Lowinger rushed forward and folded Nesanel in her arms.

"Thank you, Officer," she said in a steady voice. "You and your colleagues were wonderful! Please also convey our sincerest thanks to Sergeant Conrad."

And then she added, raising her eyes to the crowd, "And to all of you, dear friends, for what you have done for my family at this time; each of you, in so many different ways — we thank you from the bottom of our hearts."

"Everything's going to be okay now," she whispered to Nesanel. "Let's go up to the bungalow, and I'll make you a celebration breakfast."

The sound of song and dance resumed, following the parents and child all the way up the slope, and only receded when the door closed behind them.

# Chapter Fourteen

**S**huli and Avigayil wearily made their way uphill, back to the bungalow.

"I'm sleepwalking," complained Shuli. "After last night, and this homecoming, who can function normally today?"

"I know," Avigayil agreed. "I'm sure we didn't actually sleep more than two hours. Still, after breakfast I'll have to collect orders and call them in. And then, there's a plan hatching in the back of my mind."

"What now?" asked Shuli. "Why don't you just go to bed?" She yawned with abandon.

Avigayil ran her fingers through her tousled hair, and yawned in return.

"Wow, yawning's really catching! Sure, I'd love nothing better than total oblivion. But I've got a job to do. I must find out what makes Nesanel tick. D'you realize that boy was missing from before *davening* on Tuesday, until 6 A.M. today? That's twenty-four hours! It's no joke!"

"Who's laughing?" said Shuli. "Boy, I need a shower! So, what's the plan?"

"I dunno. I'm just curious to find out what's going on in that secretive mind of his. Why can't he make a single friend? Why does he hide, and spy, and throw stones? What made him run away?"

"I don't know about all the rest, but the last one's easy. He ran away because of what he did to your cabin."

"You know something? I'm not so sure he did that," said Avigayil. "Really deep down I feel that he loves the place. He's always been around, watching it change, and even helping me with odd jobs. It just doesn't make sense that he'd want to destroy it. Do you understand what I'm saying?"

People were still standing around in small clusters, discussing the early morning's events. There seemed to be a reluctance to break it up and get on with the day's regular routine. Nesanel's disappearance and his miraculous return had shaken the little community out of its humdrum existence. The whys, ifs, and buts were tossed from one to the other, but, in contrast to the night before, the free-spirited relief was evident in their nods and smiles.

Esti came running towards the two sisters.

"Nesanel's back!" she yelled.

"Who said?" Avigayil teased.

"Mommy. And you promised when I wake up he'll be home." She looked up to Avigayil, her fount of all wisdom, with unshakable trust.

"Oh, good!" said Avigayil. "We're going inside to *daven* and eat, and then I'll go for the orders. See you later, and make sure to bring your pointers!"

The morning took its usual course, and by the time she had finished with Esti, Avigayil's mind was made up. The person she had to see was Zeidy Breich.

She knocked, timidly, on the door of the bungalow next to her own, and was greeted by Mrs. Breich, who was busy cutting up vegetables.

"Something wrong with my order, Avi?" she asked.

"Oh, no! Not at all! I thought I'd like to visit with Rabbi Breich, if that's okay? I need help with something, and maybe... that is, if he's not resting or learning?"

Mrs. Breich smiled. She was the best daughter-in-law a Zeidy could wish for, Avigayil thought. Always cheerful and calm!

"Go out to the back; he'll be delighted, I'm sure. I think he's reading the Times. There are a couple of lines about Nesanel, believe it or not. Next edition they'll report about his re-appearance."

Zeidy sat in his wheelchair in the shade of a mighty oak tree. At his side they had placed a wrought-iron coffee table, on which all his *sefarim*, tapes and papers were neatly stacked. The inevitable jug of tea and a tall glass stood on a little tray near at hand.

Avigayil cleared her throat to announce her presence discreetly.

Rabbi Breich turned to her immediately. "Hello, young lady! What brings you so far from home? It's truly a day of *nissim* in Piney Hollow. *Hodu L'ashem ki tov, ki l'olom chasdo!*" he boomed.

Avigayil pulled a chair over, and smiled at the older man whom she'd known for so many summers.

"I need your help with Nesanel," she blurted out. "You've handled hundreds of boys that age, throughout your life. I know he's very different, but I think that's okay. Not everyone has to be the same. But nobody likes him, and he doesn't like anyone, either. And now look what's happened! It's bad news when a kid like that really runs away, seriously, I mean, not just to the end of the block! No?"

"Yes. It is 'bad news.' And I also think you might be able to reach him. You see, it's an ideal combination we have here. He loves the renovation project, and he gets on well with you because you do not represent a threat to him. In his own very limited way, he has managed to communicate with you, hasn't he?"

"Definitely! It's just that if I understood better where he's coming from…" Her voice trailed off.

"Well," Zeidy began, taking off his bifocals and giving them a vigorous polishing with his handkerchief, "we can only guess, and draw some possible conclusions from facts we have garnered." He placed the sparkling spectacles back on the bridge of his nose, and regarded Avigayil earnestly.

"We have a little boy who's been born to older parents. But unlike youngest little boys in similar situations, this one's without older siblings. He is the only focus of their love and care. Whatever he does, good and bad, reflects on that relationship. Do you see how that can be quite uncomfortable? All of Hashem's creatures need generous portions of care and attention to thrive, but nobody wants such concentrated, intense concern every moment of their lives. That's a lot of pressure!"

"But he was their special gift. Mrs. Lowinger was telling us all about it last night. They were about forty and fifty when he was born!" Avigayil was distraught.

"Of course! And it was a tremendous *berachah*. This is nobody's fault — not theirs and not his. It's a challenge, that's all. I remember having such cases in school. Youngsters were often embarrassed about their parents for one reason or another. Sometimes it was the way they looked, sometimes the way they talked or behaved. One boy, far above average in height and weight, never told his parents when there were parent-teacher conferences. His parents were like dwarfs, and he couldn't handle it. Now, in this case, the fact that the parents are old enough to be his grandparents might well have brought about such feelings vis-à-vis his peers. But we have more here.

"The father is a quiet, withdrawn man, a diamond cutter on 47$^{th}$ Street. He spends his entire day in his little cubicle working with his talented hands, interacting only when necessary with others. He is highly respected for his expertise. I guess he's one of the top men in his field, with a lifetime of experience. Mrs. Lowinger is a wonderful lady. Look how she's handled this whole business!" Zeidy reached for a drink. "Still, she, too, is a private, reserved person. I suspect it's a very quiet home with no young people at the Shabbos table. Nor do I see Mrs. Lowinger as a mixer in the sense of community work, committees or such. These two individuals probably find it very hard to relate to today's younger generation."

"Yeah. I can tell by the way he's dressed. So old-fashioned, and always perfect from head to toe," mentioned Avigayil.

"Another thing," Zeidy continued. "I asked Tzali why the boys kicked him out of day camp the very first day. He says Nesanel's miserable at sports; he also can't swim, by the way, and so he turned the tables on them and insisted that they didn't know the rules of baseball, they were cheating, and the kids in his New York yeshivah play much better. He made up a bunch of stories about how they all play in Little League against other yeshivos, and that they win every game. He went on and on like that. The kids weren't exactly interested in having him around after that, of course. But Tzali did say that he's very clever with his hands, and can fix most anything. He must have that from his father."

They sat quietly for a long time.

"What shall I do?" Avigayil finally asked.

"Make him happy by letting him do things he's really good at. Help him understand that he's extremely bright and capable, and also, in a real way, very special in being the *ben yachid* of such devoted parents. He must gradually learn that it's not necessary to make up stories, boast, or lash out at others, to build up one's own image. Go easy on him, Avi, because he has a real handicap."

"What do you mean, a handicap?"

"Well, in school we see all kinds of problems. The learning disabled, the children with poor motor development, some who can't manipulate their hands and feet to do what everyone takes for granted. There are children with reading problems, children with speech problems, and so on.

"And then, sometimes we see a child like Nesanel, who can't cope with social interaction. They just can't function in normal interplay. Usually they're frustrated, angry, aggressive and bossy; although I've seen the opposite too: children who shut out the world, and withdraw into themselves because they can't communicate."

Zeidy folded his paper and added, "This has become a regular teachers' in-service-training speech. What I mean to say is just that we must regard Nesanel as much in need of help as, say, another child who requires remedial work with reading. He's carrying a heavy millstone around his neck, and in fleeing he clearly signaled an S.O.S. That should be our wake-up call. Good luck, Avi! I do hope this helped some. As for myself, I'll try to knock a bit of sense into some of the boys around here. I'll also speak to the parents about how to deal with him. Can't hurt!" He chuckled.

Avigayil got up, and sighed deeply.

"It's a big assignment, but thanks a million! I hope I didn't take up too much of your time, but nobody here has worked with so many boys, and I knew where to ask. Thanks tons, Rabbi Breich; I'll let you know how it's going."

In her own bungalow, minutes later, she finally collapsed onto her bed, and almost immediately was sound asleep.

# Chapter Fifteen

**W**hat a week! thought Avigayil. Sunday she had taken orders, Monday, deliveries and pick-ups, new floor put down, Tuesday, a day never to be forgotten for the rest of her life; Wednesday, Nesanel's triumphant return, orders again, the visit with Zeidy Breich, and a trip into town with Rutti to pick up some more paint. And now, Thursday, having taken care of the pick-ups of groceries, and herself shlepping up and delivering the Schiffs' packages (since no one had come for them), here she was, painting with Nesanel.

She had offered to let him do one wall in the little broom closet, in back of the bathroom, all by himself, as a sort of experiment. If he managed to do a good job, she might let him try some more.

She kept glancing in his direction, telling herself over and over that just seeing him alive, well and happy, was the most profound feeling she'd ever experienced. Many times during the unbearable twenty-four hours, she had blamed herself and her project for his disappearance. It was heaven to watch him, private and secretive as ever, but sturdy and very real, at her side.

"I never really slept that night," he suddenly said, continuing with his work.

"Oh? Which night was that?" she asked, holding her breath.

"Not the one in the boat. The one before."

"How come?" She was careful to keep her tone casual, so as not to discourage conversation.

"Remember when you showed your mother and sister the new floor? And you said you'd start painting real early? I was hiding on the side of the cabin and I heard you." For a split second his eyes left the painting and watched her. "So I made a plan to get up here before you did. I thought maybe you would let me do some."

"That was a nice idea." Avigayil hoped she was sufficiently nonchalant.

"Yes. I never even got into pajamas."

Avigayil left her half-finished windowsill with the brush resting atop the can, and walked over to him.

"Looks good so far," she said, closely inspecting his efforts. "Great! Keep going!"

Nesanel nodded and continued.

"I got up here about five in the morning, and your door was wide open. There was paint all over the floor! It was terrible!" His face was distorted in a grimace. She thought he would burst into tears. He stopped painting and looked up at her.

"First I thought I'd go knock at your door, to get you up, but then...."

"Yes?"

"I knew you'd think I did it. *Everyone* would say I did it! Even Tzali!" He licked his lips and frowned.

"Oh, no!" exclaimed Avigayil

"Oh, *yes!*" Nesanel insisted. "'Look what that kid did now! Rotten apple! He's impossible! We've never had one like that in Piney Hollow — a *rasha*, that Nesanel.'"

The child was actually mimicking the voices of adults and children in the bungalow colony. He bent down low to do the wooden molding at the base of the wall.

Avigayil was shocked at the depth of his despair. Keep it cool, she told herself.

"Well ... whatever. You certainly should have called me."

Nesanel sighed. "I was too scared. I ran back home, took a bottle of water, two peaches and a sandwich bag stuffed with cookies. Oh, yes; and my jacket, and some change my mother keeps in a jar for the washing machine. And then, before anyone was up, I was out of here."

"Hm! On tippy-toes, no doubt. It's a wonder your mother didn't hear you," said Avigayil thoughtfully. "And I'm surprised about something else, too. Didn't anyone stop you on the way, or in the park; I mean, to ask where you're going so early in the morning, or even later in the day? You do realize, don't you, that they found you five miles from Piney Hollow?"

"Guess I was lucky," Nesanel told her with a grin. "I just walked and walked and rested and ate, and walked some more. Not one person stopped me." He straightened up and checked his handiwork carefully.

"Hey, what are all these?" He scooped up two handfuls of small pinecones, spattered with yellow paint, from behind some old pipes.

"No idea," said Avigayil. "Put them by the sink; I can use them with Esti later. Tell me, did you ever think we might be looking for you?"

"Sure," said Nesanel, "my mother…"

"Never mind your mother," Avigayil broke in. "The whole place was going crazy with worry! People called *Eretz Yisrael* to have their families and friends daven for you at the *Kosel*; not to mention yeshivos in New York, the mountains, and countless colonies and camps around here. You made all the headlines, Nesanel."

The boy shrugged.

"Do you think I did it?" he blurted out, busying himself spreading a dropcloth under the next wall.

"No." said Avigayil. "As a matter of fact, I don't. I'll tell you something, though. To be totally honest, it crossed my mind, but that was about it. It did cross my mind, but I let it go. Then I wondered if maybe Pete's still around, protesting my moving into his cabin! Or maybe someone else had it in for me …"

At the mention of Pete, Nesanel grinned.

"Anyhow, who helped you clean up?" he wanted to know.

"Manuel and Eva. It took forever!" Avigayil stopped. "Hey! I just had a major idea! Let's take a break; come!"

"Now?"

"Yes, right this minute. I'll lock up."

Nesanel followed Avigayil, who was already speeding down towards the main house. She seemed to be taking it for granted that Nesanel was coming after her.

They found Eva and Manuel busy in the long-neglected *shul*.

"Hi!" called Avigayil.

"Hi!" They both answered in unison, looking up with bright, smiling faces. Without much to share in the way of conversation, they had somehow become good friends.

"Sorry to interrupt," sputtered Avigayil. "But, Manuel, how happen big mess my house?" She spread her arms wide, palms up and raised her eyebrows.

"Sure. No problem." Manuel's grin now stretched ear to ear. "Three, four, maybe eight mouses play baseball."

"What?" shrieked Avigayil. Nesanel stood nearby, transfixed.

"Mouses come, run, play, paint fall floor, big mess!"

Eva nodded earnestly. But then she amended:

"No, no mouses." She made swirling gestures with her hands as if she were drawing in the air. Her black eyes sparkled with the fun of it. She said a few words in Spanish, and Manuel produced a scrap of paper and a pen. Quickly, Eva drew what was clearly a pair of bushy-tailed squirrels, followed by a small army of wiry little chipmunks with bold black and white stripes along their sides and faces.

Avigayil and Nesanel stared at her.

Encouraged now, she added overturned paint cans and widening puddles of paint to her cartoon.

Manuel beamed at his wife.

"Good, no? Eva good pictures!" He pointed to his brain to show how smart she was.

"Eva VERY good; excellent!" said Avigayil.

Nesanel dug in his pocket and showed them one of the paint-spattered pinecones, holding it up for their inspection.

"Yes! Yes! Right. Mouses play baseball. Me put many balls in bathroom closet," Manuel reported proudly.

"Mouses love this," he pointed to the cone. "Take from Piney Wood, much fun!"

"Thanks tons! You're the best!" cried Avigayil. "Come, Nesanel. Let's show this drawing to Mrs. Brinkman." She felt like a million dollars.

By the time they got back to the cabin, Esti was waiting for them. Addressing Nesanel, almost as an equal, Avigayil said,

"Go paint the next wall; if you want to, that is. And let's have all those pinecones for her math lesson, please."

The heat wave had finally broken, and although there wasn't any sign of rain, a gentle wind caressed the tall grasses of the meadow and ruffled Esti's hair, which today, for a change, she wore open and loose. She seemed to have gotten dressed by herself, judging by the deep purple skirt, orange top, worn back to front, and bright red socks. Avigayil gave her a great, warm bear hug.

"Math first today," she said. "Look what we have here for you. These are what squirrels use to play baseball. People call them pinecones. Anyway, let's do some adding and subtracting."

After a while she decided to change tactics.

"You know what? We're going to do the same thing now, without these. Here, hide them under the picnic table in the grass. Let's see if you can do these sums in your head. And then..." she looked at Esti with huge eyes, "then, if we don't need them anymore for lessons, I'll help you make a pinecone chain for your *succah* at home."

"Today?" asked Esti.

"Sunday," Avigayil replied, "maybe. Now, use your head, okay? Two minus one."

Furtively, Esti's eyes swiveled to see under the table.

"Uh-uh. That's a no-no! No peeking," said Avigayil.

"Can I use my fingers?"

"Only if you can't do it any other way. Close your eyes for a moment and think about the pinecones. Imagine we had two of them lying here, and we took one away."

Esti screwed her eyes shut tight.

"One?" she ventured.

"Hurray!" shouted Avigayil. "And three plus two?"

"Three, four, five," Esti whispered to herself. "Five!" she yelled out loud.

"Genius!" crowded Avi. The lesson was going swimmingly. So far it had been a glorious day, mouses and pinecones, painting and math, Nesanel and Esti — what happiness! And this afternoon, Tzali had promised to do the ceilings, just in time for Tatty and Bubby's visit tomorrow.

# Chapter Sixteen

'**G**OLD TREASURES' was the name of the store, painted in metallic gold on a royal blue background. The weather-beaten sign, suspended from a metal pole, hung above the door, much like those found in England over the entrances of old inns and taverns. This is what Bubby explained as she and Avigayil entered to the pleasant, tinkling sound of the bell on the opening door.

"Everything here is second-hand," whispered Avigayil. "But it's a great place. Everyone says so."

A rosy-cheeked woman, perhaps in her late fifties, with thick, gray hair cut short, and sparkling glasses, was busily dusting little china figurines and vases. She wore a sweater in heathery blue, a gray skirt, and a pair of no-nonsense gray shoes.

"Good afternoon," said Bubby. "What a beautiful shop! And air-conditioned, thank goodness."

"Hello, there. Thank you for the compliment. My name is Betty Gold, and I hope you'll find what you're after. Do walk around and browse. The furniture's in the next room; that's my husband Sam's domain."

Everything was displayed to great advantage, with the sun streaming in from the two large front windows and reflected in myriad facets of glass, crystal, china, and mirrors.

"I noticed too the English touch outside, what with the sign and the deep flower boxes along the windows. How charming!"

Bubby's English accent got more and more pronounced as she took it all in.

"Oh, yes. And you're right. My in-laws came from London, and we visited there quite often. I always admired the way they do their shops, so when we opened here, several years ago, we tried to get that sort of atmosphere in our place. They call it ambience these days, I believe. You must be English yourself?"

"Yes, I am that, and my name is Babsie Kaplan. This is my Yankee granddaughter, Avigayil. She's come into a little money, quite unexpectedly, and she's decided to do up a very old, ram-shackle hut, on the property of Piney Hollow Bungalow Colony. I suppose you know the place?"

"Oh, sure! Some of their regulars make a point of stepping in every summer. It's a nice bunch up there." Mrs. Gold resumed her dusting, and continued, "So if you need any help, please call me. All prices should be clearly marked, but you know we may have slipped up somewhere. And congratulations, dear, on your enterprise. What fun! I do believe I'm jealous!"

She waved her feathered duster and bustled off.

They spent a wonderful hour and a half, and it was only when they were about ready to leave that Avigayil spotted the rocking chair. It was made of oak and cane, in perfect condition, the curved arms and high back polished to a rich, warm sheen — truly a 'Gold Treasure.' Sam Gold, who had patiently answered all their questions, explained that he had bought this chair at an estate sale, from the children of the original owner. He proudly showed them a wooden floor lamp with a honey-colored silk shade. It was this lamp that had always been placed alongside the rocking chair. They 'belonged,' and the Kaplans saw he was right. The lamp was immediately plugged into an outlet and switched on. It cast a cozy, amber glow.

"Perfect!" pronounced Bubby. "For when I come and visit. But are you sure that's what *you* want, Avi, a grandma's rocking chair?"

"Absolutely! Positively!" said Avigayil dreamily, her face glowing. "It's to curl up and read in when it's pouring outside. You'll see, Mommy will sew me a pillow and maybe one for the back. Though I don't want to hide the beautiful cane. Oh, I *love* it."

She checked the price of both the chair and lamp and wrote them on a notepad.

"Would you please hold these for me for a day or two? I need a few more things, and I'll be back. I promise."

Mr. Gold, white moustache fairly bristling, withdrew some professional-looking labels with strings from the pocket of his blue denim work apron.

"No problem," he told her with a smile.

'Hold one week for Kaplans,' he wrote in spidery green letters, and knotted the tags around the furniture.

"Come in whenever you want, and I'm sure we can help you find most anything you'll be needing. We'll give you a good deal, too. It's not often that we do business with such a young, but very mature, entrepreneur! Thank you, madam!" He executed a gracious bow in her direction.

Bubby, exuberant, drove them home.

"I haven't had such fun in ages," she said. "And you! I'll let you in on a secret, Avi. Part of the fun was watching you."

Avigayil looked at her questioningly. "Watching me?"

"Exactly! It's seeing the change. When you left New York at the end of June, you were a closed book. Never to me, that's true, but to the world at large. Today, four weeks later, you're able to communicate easily and naturally, with all kinds of people. It's like day and night! A veritable miracle!"

Avigayil knew she was blushing. She also knew that Bubby had a point. She smiled when she recalled the night before her first food-order collection, when she had practiced opening conversations and how to beat a hasty retreat as soon as she could. In the meantime she had learned to deal with all types of workers in connection with the cabin, and to negotiate on her own with numerous stores. She had had dealings with Manuel and Eva, the Brinkmans, Tzali and Rutti, and even Esti, Nesanel and their parents. True, she still wasn't like Shuli, in the thick of peer society, but then she scarcely wanted that. She had come a long way.

Monday she was back at the Golds. Betty was busy with a young couple who was examining a small curio cabinet.

Sam was happy to help her.

"I'm going with the rocking chair and lamp," Avigayil told him joyously, "and here are the other things I need." She handed him a short list, and he read it, his hand trembling slightly: three stools to fit under ledge, clock, row of pegs for back of door. At the bottom she had written the measurements, height of ledge, etc.

Sam was in his element. Within half an hour, he had made her the delighted owner of a large wood-framed clock with Roman numerals, four wooden stools with backs ("they came in a set, and I'll throw one in for free,") and a handsome board with bright brass pegs for jackets and such.

Betty, whose customer had just left, came through the swinging half-door to join them. She was wearing the same cardigan, and her cheeks were as rosy as ever.

Avigayil pointed to her new acquisitions.

"What do you think? Do you like these?" she asked.

"Yes, I do! Wonderful! Isn't it amazing how, in this limited amount of space, we can almost always come up with what people are looking for! Are you all done, then? We'd love to come and see it when it's finished." And then she added, "We've heard about your special project from someone who was very involved in the search for that missing boy. You've met Jerry McDavid, right? He's always in and out of this store. He likes antiques and knick-knacks, and he also happens to like my coffee and home-made oatmeal cookies. Anyhow, when I told him you'd been here with your grandma, he couldn't stop talking about you, your renovation, and especially about how you're so good with kids. Even with one who presents difficulties, as this one certainly did."

She hesitated a moment, as if there were more, but she wasn't quite sure how to begin. Avigayil instinctively turned to Mr. Gold.

"Jerry's the young police officer. He seemed very nice, and I know that after Nesanel was found, he stayed around to chat with Tzali, the owners' nephew. He must have been the one who told Jerry all our secrets!"

"Tell me, Avigayil, would you mind if we ask you something? Have you got the extra few minutes?" Betty Gold sounded anxious, and there was a sense of pleading in her tone.

Avigayil checked her watch. Rutti would be out in front in fifteen minutes. She smiled. "I have a quarter of an hour," she said truthfully.

"Okay, that'll do." Betty rushed to the front of the store and hung the 'CLOSED' sign outside.

"Let's sit," she said, and they did, in three second-hand arm-chairs. By now, Avigayil's curiosity was piqued. In the short time she had known these people she had come to like and respect them, and she wondered what they wanted of her.

"You see, it's like this," Betty began. "We have a son and daughter-in-law who live ten minutes from here by car. He's a teacher in the high school in town, and she's the school nurse in the local elementary school. They have five children. The old-est is a boy, who's eleven, then there are three girls, ages eight, six and four, and the baby is a boy of six months. They are dar-ling kids, and — well, you know grandmothers," she said with a shy smile and a shrug. "For us, they can do no wrong. So here's our quandary. The wonderful four-year-old girl is a Downs Syndrome child."

At this point, Sam broke in. "She's no trouble and good as only a Gold can be. You know, 'Good as gold'? Still, her mom's got just two hands, and we're concerned. And it's not only for her mother, either, but many's the time when the other children need attention and can't get it. During the school year, every-one's at school, little Rebecca's in her special kindergarten, and the baby goes to a sitter. But come summertime, they're all home and clamoring for family hikes, swimming, picnics and what-have-you."

"To cut a long story short," continued Betty, "we wanted to ask you whether you'd be willing to have Rebecca with you, say, twice a week, for two hours." She swallowed hard. "There, I've said it. But I should also add that they're not as Orthodox as all of you at Piney Hollow. They basically keep Kosher and observe Passover and the High Holidays; whatever they don't do is our fault. We raised them this way. So, oh, Avigayil, would you try? Just try?"

Avigayil looked at the two, and her heart went out to them. "B...b...but I haven't a clue how to handle something like this," she stammered.

"Sandy, our daughter-in-law, would have to meet with you first, of course, and tell you all about the child. For her, a short break like this, twice a week, would be a gift from heaven. Needless to say we'd pay you."

"You know what?" added Sam. "Think about it, and talk to your mother. You don't have to give an answer right now. Look, if you're scared of it, we'd understand perfectly. No pressure. Just promise to give it a thought. How's that?"

෧ౚౖఄ ෧ౚౖఄ ෧ౚౖఄ

A week later, the clock hung on the wall, ticking away the hours, the stools stood neatly tucked under the pumpkin-colored ledge, the pegs adorned the back of the door, the rocking chair dominated the room with the beautiful lamp just behind it, and Rebecca Gold, blue-eyed, black-haired and 'pleasantly plump,' sat at the picnic table with Esti Neufeld, both of them swinging their short legs like mad and giggling.

෧ౚౖఄ ෧ౚౖఄ ෧ౚౖఄ

Mr. Kaplan had called up to say that Bubby wasn't coming for Shabbos this week. She had a miserable cold, accompanied by low temperature, and all she wanted was to burrow under piles of cozy blankets, in her own familiar bed.

Avigayil was very disappointed. She had looked forward so much to showing Bubby how far she had come. But Tatty, when he came, made up for everything. He was suitably impressed, and when she showed him her expense account, and the balance still in savings, he thought she had done just fine. A graphic rendering of Manuel and Eva's explanation of the paint incident brought tears of laughter. Mommy had, of course, told him all about Nesanel's escapade, but he wanted to hear every little detail again from Avigayil.

"Does he go to day camp now?" he wanted to know.

"Well, in a way he does. I mean, there's been some improvement. He goes to the learning session every morning for an hour and a half. It's too much, at this point, to expect him to stay for sports and stuff. There's still quite a bit of tension there. But I think... I hope... maybe... one step at a time. Between you and me, Zeidy Breich is accomplishing things behind the scenes. He can't work with Nesanel, but he is making a difference with some of the boys. And Nesanel is up here with me quite a lot, and also with Tzali."

"But where does Tzali find the time?" asked Mr. Kaplan

"Tzali's one in a million. He's the most laid-back person I know. Even when he's loaded down with jobs and way behind schedule, you'd never guess. He lets Nesanel hang around the workshop and watch or help. Sometimes he takes him along in the truck. There's no heavy pressure or strain with him...ever! And I think that's exactly why it works."

Mr. Kaplan smiled. "It looks like we have a budding psychologist here. You're probably right on the mark. Okay, so when's the *Chanukas HaBayis?*"

Avigayil stared at him.

"That's the greatest idea, Ta. I love it! All the painting and renovating is finished. In the Nine Days we can't do much, anyhow, so ... how about after the Three Weeks are over? By that time it should be all ready. What exactly do we have to do for something like that?"

Mr. Kaplan mulled this over for a minute.

"You know, I'm not quite sure. Let me talk to Rav Rosener this week and get some answers. This is a rather special situation. There may be some differences between your palace here and, for example, buying a house. Hmmm... interesting! Now, when's this little Rebecca coming? I sure want to meet her!"

"She's here the two mornings I don't have anything to do with orders, Tuesdays and Fridays. But Esti comes earlier for her lessons. Listen to this, Ta! Today, we're working on the last Hebrew sheet she has to do for the whole summer! We're miles ahead! I'll have most of August to do whatever I choose. Isn't that fantastic?"

Mr. Kaplan shook his head in wonder.

"If she's promoted this fall, I'll *shep* more *nachas* than her own parents," he declared. "Oh! Here comes Esti herself."

He turned to the little girl, and bent down to her eye-level.

"Is Avi nice to you?"

Esti nodded, and stuck her finger into her mouth.

"If she's ever mean, you just tell me, 'cause I'm her Tatty, and I'll make her stop!" He gave her his best 'President-of-the-*shul*' smile, gently tugged at one of her sprouting pigtails, and headed down to the *Beis HaMidrash*.

༺ ༺ ༺

'Shefford,' performed that Sunday evening in Camp Zimra, was a major success. Shuli and Avigayil watched the performance, while their mother directed and supervised all things connected with costumes behind the scenes.

"Now that I've seen this," said Shuli in the car on the way home, late at night, "I want to read more about it. It's an amazing story." She yawned. "Your costumes were perfect, Ma! The girl who played Dr. Grunfeld looked absolutely royal! No wonder all the kids nicknamed her 'The Queen.' "

"What's the next play about?" Avigayil wanted to know.

"In a way, that's going to be more of a challenge. It's some kind of fantasy thing, historical and then going all the way down to our times. Ugh!" Mrs. Kaplan sounded drained.

"Oh, Avi, I forgot to tell you: Tatty called this morning. Rav

Rosener said to go right ahead with a *Chanukas HaBayis*. But, because it's only a rented, temporary place, you can't say the *berachah* of *Shehecheyanu*. Also, girls are allowed to put up a *mezuzah*. Isn't that nice? You can do your own thing up to the very end, but again, without a *berachah*. By the way, that's for all bungalows; they have to have *mezuzos*, but we don't say the *berachah*."

"Oh, great! Who do we invite, Ma?"

"I didn't tell you the best part yet; hold on! Tatty wants to bring all the *nash* from New York — every little thing! He refuses to have me bother here. This is supposed to be my vacation, so how could I argue with that? Which means you can have whomever you want. Tishah B'Av is Tuesday of next week, so let's have it the Sunday after. Bubby will be here by then for *her* two weeks. Perfect, no?"

Avigayil curled up in her back seat. Ta's the greatest! And Mommy too. They're so happy with me, she thought. In her mind she went over the short list of things that still had to be taken care of. Curtains with little rings, the kind you pull open and shut. Ceiling lights, to be fixed up and covered with glass shades (courtesy of Tzali, hopefully!) Both of these could be seen to right after Tishah B'Av, before the party.

Shuli, in her corner, made her own plans. Maybe she'd put on a song and dance performance with her six-year-olds. Or maybe a huge box with loads of little gifts, wrapped up in layers and layers, from all the older girls? A speech?

"Avi, you'll have to make a speech," she remarked.

"Oh, yes?" Avi hadn't been paying attention and was taken by surprise.

"Ma, tell her!"

"It would be very nice, Avi, but only if you want to." Mrs. Kaplan refused to act as a referee at one-thirty in the morning.

# Chapter Seventeen

*Bubby Babsie's Thoughts and Reflections*
(A chapter all to herself — she deserves it!)

**M**y cold's all better, and I was happy to come to Piney Hollow with Velvel on Friday. Tuesday was Tishah B'Av, and I fasted quite well, thank G-d. When that day rolls around, I always remember my childhood; it never fails. Tishah B'Av in Commercial Road of London's East End. When Solly, *a'h*, and the boys were in *shul* with Daddy, Mum gathered us around — Daisy and me, that is, because by then Doreen was gone — and we said *Eichah* at night and the *Kinos* in the morning. We sat on low, upside-down boxes from the cellar. Daisy and I wore our gym shoes from school, but

Mum had on her old, shabby beige felt slippers. It seems like yesterday!

And now, I'm sitting here Sunday afternoon, August 9th, basking in the sun, and watching it all. Commercial Road is more than half a century in the past, but the chief actor in today's drama, Avigayil Kaplan, and for that matter, her sister Shuli, are as surely Mummy and Daddy's emissaries to this new world as arrows, shot straight and true from the bow.

This is a grand, special day. It's at times like today that I miss my Menasheh most. How he would have *kvelled* to see his grandchildren on an occasion such as this. But, I have to be grateful to Hashem that He has spared me and given me the blessing of long years.

Velvel had the car loaded down with pies and cookies, sweets and nuts, potato chips and popcorn — enough to feed a regiment! Early this morning, we all worked together and set up everything on the picnic table, and inside on the two long counters. Only the drinks had to be bought here, and Tzali brought those along in his truck.

We're lucky to have such fine weather today. It's hot, but there's a nice breeze every once in a while. People keep coming, admiring the cabin, tasting the goodies, and having a wonderful time with their friends.

I see the Golds over there, with their children and grandchildren. Little Rebecca's already at home here. Avi uses flash cards to teach her the colors and the names of the objects in the pictures. They dress and undress a special doll that's the most be'velcro'd, buttoned-up, zippered play thing I ever saw. Esti plays with it, too, and most of the time, that's exactly what they do — play and enjoy! It's just incredible! They all adore Avi, and I saw the Golds giving her a simply lovely old mirror for her new 'bungalow.'

The two couples I didn't recognize were introduced to me by

the Brinkmans. These are their partners in the Colony. The hand-crafted 'woodsy' *mezuzah* case Avi used earlier to affix her *mezuzah* came from one of them, all the way from *Eretz Yisrael*.

Velvel gave Avi a cell phone. "More for my own peace of mind," he said. "This way she can always be in touch." I feel good about that, too; this place *is* a bit secluded.

Look! Eva and Manuel all spruced up in their Sunday best! I suppose they're feeling a little shy about mingling with the rest, but they wouldn't miss it for the world!

Shuli put on a lovely performance with her Day Camp tots. She's such a good sport! All this fuss about her sister, but she's whole-heartedly unselfish in her joy. I can tell it's real, all the way through. She's sparkling!

Here come the Neufelds, hoisting a long, flat parcel wrapped in paper, obviously finger-painted. Modern art — must be Esti's own work! This is great fun! Avi's unwrapping it ... and it's a big cork bulletin board. That will be perfect to display all the kids' work. So much love and thought has gone into these gifts!

Oh, dear! What's happening? My eyes are misting up. Surely it's not my cold coming back! Where's my hanky? Let me blow my nose before the tears come rolling down these cheeks. I'm turning into a real sentimental old fuddy-duddy.

Now take the Brinkmans: there's practicality and good sense. They gave Avi a new lock for that cabin door. And Tzali and Rutti, too — a good-sized sturdy first-aid kit, always to be kept on the premises. It's clear all these people have faith in the future of Avi's venture.

Oh, my goodness! A small microwave oven from the Lowingers. Pizza and grilled cheese sandwiches, I can just see it! Such a lady, that Bas Sheva! I pray that Hashem should give her much *nachas* from that child. Where on earth is he anyway? Squatting behind some rock, no doubt, or...

Why, the police are here! There's a young officer, with flaming red hair, rocking back and forth on the balls of his feet, keeping an eye on things. How strange! But somehow, he seems to 'belong.' He's deep in conversation with Sam Gold and, I notice, polishing off great numbers of cookies at the same time.

Can it really be true that our Avi has brought all these so very different people together — our young recluse? Our loner by choice?

Hush! They're calling for quiet. I suppose Avi will say a few words. I see them pushing Zeidy Breich's wheelchair up front, so he can hear her better.

*"Dear Friends!"* (Here she goes!)

*"I just can't say everything that's in my heart. But I want to say thank you to Hashem for having brought it all about. Thank you to my Bubby Babsie's older sister, Doreen, a'h, who started the whole thing. I hope she'd be happy with what came of her generosity. I hope, too, that what I chose would have pleased my great-grandmother, for whom I'm named. I can't mention everyone who helped me, but a most special Hakaras HaTov belongs to Tzali, Rutti and the Brinkmans.*

*"It started out as a vague dream for myself, and maybe for something more. It's becoming that with your friendship and Hashem's constant help. My Bubby, father, mother and Shuli are with me all the way. I'll try not to let them down.*

*"And now, a surprise gift from my mother; I mean that — total surprise! I have no idea what this is."*

Avi is opening another package. Oh! How beautiful! It's a framed oil painting of the cabin. Sue really captured the essence of it, nestled in the grass, and backed up by Piney Woods. It's a little jewel!

"Oh, Ma! It's gorgeous!" She's holding it up for everyone to see.

"Boy, did I ever have a hard time keeping this secret," says

Sue, laughing. "I had to steal moments when you were in town with Rutti, and then hide it at the Breichs! It's to take home to New York, and to look at whenever you feel 'homesick.' That'll keep you going until next summer; unless *Mashiach* comes first, *b'ezras Hashem*."

My daughter-in-law's quite a girl. Talented in so many ways, but above all, she's a good, giving, caring individual. I'm blessed with her — truly!

Here I go again, sniffing away! But no one's noticing. They're all telling Avi how well she spoke, and oohing and aahing over Sue's work of art; and so they might! Otherwise, everyone's tucking in to their heart's delight. The food seems to hit the spot.

Is that who I think it is, coming up the slope? Yes, indeed! Nesanel Lowinger, 'Dennis the Menace,' has come bearing a gift. Time bomb? Sling-shot extraordinaire? He looks flushed, as if he's exerted himself powerfully, with whatever this package contains. Maybe it was the wrapping of it? It's bulky and packed in thick, brown paper, taped again and again all around. He's labored over this, poor thing! He cares!

In front of all these people, he walks bravely up to Avi and thrusts it into her hands. And then, before she can say a single word — he bolts. They call after him, but he can't face this part. It took all of his resolve to come thus far.

They let him go. He'll surely find a place to hide from which he can watch. Avi painstakingly unwraps the parcel. The contents are lovingly folded in soft cloth. And then, held up to the light — a beautiful wooden sign. On it, in cursive writing, are the words, 'AVI'S PLACE.' Looking closer, it becomes clear that these words are spelled out by, incredibly, two long brown shoelaces, meticulously glued into place. The plaque is varnished and shellacked to a bright gloss, over and over the laces, until they take on a real existence of their own. A rope is drawn through two neatly drilled holes, to hang on the door in place of Pete's old proof of ownership.

Avi can't speak. She looks questioningly at Tzali, and he nods. He's been in cahoots with this boy; the many hours Nesanel spends in that workshop bear beautiful fruit.

"It was his own idea, and mostly even his own work. He's a very handy kid," booms Tzali. "He appropriated, shall we say, those laces, the day you left the workmen to install your new linoleum. He'd already begun work on the board that very morning. Great job, isn't it?"

Avi's walking over to the door, and almost reverently replaces the old sign with the new.

Oh, my! Now they're all clapping. I fervently hope the child is watching from somewhere. It's nothing short of a rousing, unanimous vote of approval! Bravo, Nesanel! What a moving ending to an afternoon I'll treasure forever. All I can do now is echo Doreen's words: Go, Avi — GO!

# *Epilogue*

**A**fter supper Avigayil and Bubby were sitting on the glider rehashing the day's events. Avigayil cradled a small, exquisite vase in her cupped hands. It was Bubby's gift to remind her of Abby Silver, and her love of little posies. Avi would always keep it filled, and give it a place of honor in her cabin.

"Guess what Nesanel told me Friday!" Avigayil said. "He told me that Yanky Neufeld asked him to come swimming on Sunday, and he'd teach him to put his face and head in the water. He promised him, 'Once you can do that, swimming's a cinch! And best of all, next time you run away, at least we won't have to worry that you drowned!'

"Nesanel is so keyed up about the prospect, he can't sleep. Should he, shouldn't he? I think he feels it would be the first step to capitulating. Like a white flag!"

"What did you advise?"

"I said, 'Good idea! There's another hot spell coming up. The pool's the perfect place to be.' Well, we'll soon see what happens."

They rocked in friendly silence, each pursuing her own train of thought.

"Bubby," Avigayil asked after a while, "have you no idea who it could have been that kept in touch with Doreen all these years? How did she really know about our names and where we lived? I mean, in three different countries and everything!"

Bubby continued rocking; then, turning towards Avigayil, she said, "For a girl as intelligent as you are, I'm really surprised you never guessed. Why, of course it was me! Or, using correct grammar as we were taught in Prince Edward Primary School, 'It was I, my dear.'"